ELSKER

THE ELSKER SAGA: BOOK ONE

ST BENDE

First electronic publication: 2013, Entranced Publishing LLC
First print publication: 2013, ST Bende

Edited by Eden Plantz
Cover Art by Cali MacKay;
Snowflakes by Nyorai/Meldir/brusheezy.com

This book is a work of fiction. Names, characters, places, and incidents either are products of the author's imagination or are used fictitiously. Any resemblance to actual persons, living or dead, events, or locales is entirely coincidental.

DEDICATION

To my three boys --
I wished for you upon a star,
and all my dreams came true.

CONTENTS

THE PROPHECY OF RAGNAROK

With the death of Balder, the powers of darkness will burst from their tethers. Jotunheim shall crack open; a terrible frost shall suffocate all things good. The great beast will attack, the wicked ship sail, and the light of Asgard will dim evermore. Fire shall consume the earth and Darkness shall swallow the sky. No one, God or Mortal, can survive the travesty of Ragnarok.

-Prophecy of The Norns

ST BENDE

1. TRAVEL

I MOVED FASTER THAN a salmon down a chute in bear season. I had to. If the giant wolf biting at my heels didn't kill me, then the tree-trunk of a snake twining between my feet was going to finish the job. I pumped my legs harder, exerting every modicum of strength I had left, and in the process, I stepped on the snake's head. It hissed, a guttural reverberation bouncing around the darkness. I pushed harder. My chest burned, but I'd managed to put a little space between my attackers and me. I could hear the wolf's angry growl, but I didn't look back. I couldn't spare the movement.

Since it was pitch black, I couldn't see what I was running towards, and I certainly didn't see the fissures beginning to form in the dirt beneath my Nikes. My size six sneaker slid into one and I could hear the crack of my ankle breaking before I hit the damp earth. The chasm was getting bigger and soon my whole leg slipped through. My fingernails clung to the soil as it separated from itself, and I felt the chill creep over the ground as the terrible frost settled like a blanket onto everything it could reach. I started to shake -- it would be death by freezing, then. But I knew chilled human wouldn't be the worst thing the wolf and snake had eaten that day.

"Earth to Kristia! Hello? Are you even listening?" I rubbed my eyes and focused on the frowning face of my best friend since kindergarten. A sprightly brunette, Ardis was everything I wasn't -- adventurous, perky, self-confident. And at the moment, highly irritated.

"Sorry," I shook off the remnants of last night's bad dream. Ardis Behrman didn't often grace our hometown of Nehalem, Oregon. Three hundred residents and a solitary stoplight didn't hold much excitement for a girl studying acting at NYU. I treasured any conversation we had that didn't require text or Skype.

"Vision?" She cocked her head.

"Hardly. Just tired. Nightmare last night."

"The weird one about the animals hunting you down?" Ardis wrinkled her nose.

"That's the one." My favorite grandmother's dark stories from the North were never far from my subconscious. I never understood how any woman in her right mind could lovingly recount the end of the mythological Norse world to an eight-year-old girl. Mormor always had a wicked sense of humor, so I liked to think her intentions were good. Or maybe she suffered from a touch of the crazy. The fact that, at twenty, I still had vivid nightmares about Ragnarok; well, that spoke more about my own sensitivities than anything else. They were just stories.

"That dream's just creepy, Kristia."

"Tell me about it."

"So." Ardis rested her hands on the table. The metallic blue sparkles on her nails caught the light of the coffee shop where we'd had countless heart-to-hearts. "What's new in Nehalem?"

I stopped just short of rolling my eyes. "Good one Ardis." Nothing changed around here but the weather, and even that was freakishly consistent.

"And the University of the Pacific Northwest?"

"You mean High School, Part Deux?"

"C'mon, it can't be that bad."

"You do realize you're the only member of our graduating class who doesn't go there, right? The only one who isn't going to end up married to someone they've known since kindergarten. And spend eternity working in the boring log mill or tourist traps." It would be the latter for me. My parents' antique shop was popular with the summer crowd and I was expected to begin fulltime work when I graduated. Not exactly the stuff of dreams.

"If you're that bored, don't just sit around waiting for something to happen to you -- go out and grab it."

"It's not that easy," I mumbled. Ardis was one of those people to whom good things came naturally. She didn't understand that life didn't just fall into place for the rest of us.

I glanced up as our waitress set two steaming mugs on

our table with a little too much force. I raised my eyebrows. "Is everything all right today, Susan?" My voice strained with the effort of false nicety. In our twelve years of school together, Susan had always treated me like a social pariah. Clearly nothing had changed since graduation. I may not have been well bred, but I *was* well raised. I pasted on my best fake smile, though after enduring a lifetime of whispers and stares I had a very low tolerance for rudeness. It was my absolute pet peeve.

I held Susan's glare with my own pleasant look until she scurried back to the kitchen, obviously uncomfortable. Well, I was used to that.

"Sorry, what were you saying? You don't think it's easy to change your life? You only think that because you've never tried." Ardis sipped impatiently at her latte, the unofficial beverage of our rain-drenched town. "Look, Kristia, you're my best friend and I think you rock. But is sitting around Nehalem for the rest of your life really going to make you happy? Really?" Score one, Behrman.

The minute she said it I was transported from the rainy-small-town coffee shop to a dreary house on the edge of Nehalem.

Rain was falling outside the thin windows and the air was damp with the faint scent of mildew. A cleaning caddy was at my feet -- I must have just scrubbed the toilets, judging from the smell of bleach, and I was folding laundry while the television droned in the background. When the boredom consumed me, I crossed to a coffee table where I idly fingered my one indulgence in an otherwise uneventful life: my subscription to Travel Magazine. The cover boasted an Irish castle sitting in a brilliant green field of clovers.

4

My heart tugged -- in my vision I was thirty years old and I'd never even been on an airplane. I forced myself back to the coffee shop, where Ardis was watching me closely.

"What did you see?"

"Absolutely nothing," I shook my head. I was resolute. My life was not going to turn out that way. It was one vision that could never come true. I drew a breath. I was twenty years old. Time to choose the path I wanted my life to take. There was a whole world out there -- what was keeping me from living in it? From living, period? "I still have one year of college left. I'm not spending it here. Not anymore."

"Awesome," Ardis nodded her approval. "So what are you gonna do?"

"I'm..." I was at a loss. I hadn't thought that far ahead. "Well..." Then it came to me. "Got it! UPN has study abroad. The deadline isn't for another three weeks. I'll spend senior year somewhere totally different -- somewhere people don't know anything about me."

"Bravo," Ardis clapped loudly, to Susan's chagrin. She glared at us from behind the counter. "So where do you want to go?"

I had to think. Now that I'd made the decision to leave the country, where should I go? I thought about the book on my nightstand -- a Jane Austen classic. Those ladies seemed to be enjoying themselves, in their own angsty way. They certainly had a good time romping through the

English Countryside. I had my answer. Once I'd made up my mind, I pictured something altogether different.

I was on a big fancy jet, flying towards Europe. A flight attendant was handing me a coke with a lemon wedge and I was staring out the window at the endless, green meadows passing beneath. The businessman to my left was reading the Wall Street Journal, *and the one across the aisle was immersed in the* London Times.

Oh, crimeney. What had I gotten into now?

"So where are you going?" Like always, Ardis glossed right over my little mind trip. Bless her heart.

"England. No, Wales." A few miles closer to home might make it seem a little less scary. I dropped my head in my hands. Darned hallucinations. I hadn't had one in months, and I'd just had two in as many minutes. It was with no small amount of pleasure that I took the visions back.

The three hundred townsfolk of Nehalem whispered about my "handicap" when they thought I wasn't listening -- actually, it was a mental problem. It was generally accepted that I was two trees short of a forest. Thanks to some glitch in my brain, I saw random flashes of the future against my will. I'd been in two minor car accidents, failed four midterm exams, and had to avoid competitive sports entirely, all because I saw stuff at lousy times. This wouldn't have been so much of a disability if I could have seen the winning lotto numbers, or even just the location of the radar-cops who hid along the 101. But to date, my premonitions had yielded zero useful tidbits. I saw the mundane, ranging from my mom doing a load of laundry to

Ardis painting her toes fire-engine red. I was the world's most useless psychic.

"Wales it is then," Ardis nodded her head firmly. "Now we just have to make sure you actually get on that plane."

"What's that supposed to mean?"

"Oh, let me think Miss Art History major -- because that's not the perfect degree to take over the family antique shop or anything." Ardis jabbed me with a sparkly fingernail.

"It just so happens that I like art." I did.

"True or false? You come home every weekend to study instead of staying on campus and actually having a good time."

"I have a good time at home!" My protest fell on deaf ears.

"True or false? You've literally never been more than ninety miles from the spot you were born."

"Well that's just because--"

"Buzz, time's up!" Ardis giggled. "Kristia Homebody Tostenson, you win one personal escort to the airport to make sure you actually do something exciting for once in your life!"

"Fine," I nudged her with my boot. "But you're going to miss me when I'm gone."

"You know it."

****

Nine months and one very bumpy plane ride later, I was seriously questioning this whole big-adventure plan. I was thousands of miles from home, hurtling through the air in a bouncing box. How exactly was this a good idea?

"Fasten your seatbelts and return your seats and tray tables to their full and upright positions as we begin our descent into London, Heathrow. Weather is a pleasant fifty-five degrees with a light rain." Thank heavens. The turbulent flight was almost over. "Seat up, Miss," tusked the flight attendant as I adjusted my chair guiltily.

"Sorry Ma'am," I murmured to her retreating back, small-town manners a compulsive response. I leaned over to peer at the approaching countryside. Green pastures dotted with tiny sheep stretched as far as I could see, with farmhouses lining the landscape at sporadic intervals. The green was a stark contrast to the gray of the sky. I was staring down the barrel of a very soggy year.

This suited me just fine. I liked rain. The summer sun did not favor the pale. Besides, cold weather gave me an excuse to sit in my favorite reading chair with my beverage of choice -- Earl Grey, one milk, two sugars. As we bounced through the sky I tried to focus on what kinds of tea they'd have at my home for the next nine months, Cardiff University in Wales. Lots of fancy ones, I was sure. If I survived this flight, I'd graduate in nine months time.

Hopefully, my History of Art degree would earn me a spot as junior curator at a museum. For the first time in my life, I was about to step into the great unknown. The best thing about the unknown was that nobody knew me there -- at Cardiff I wouldn't be Crazy Kristia, the poor, weird girl who saw things. Maybe for once, I could just be another coed. It was my fervent wish to blend into the scenery.

I took a deep breath to soothe my sudden panic as the flight attendants opened the doors and my fellow passengers rose to exit the airplane. The great unknown suddenly seemed very scary.

****

I stood across the street from the Heathrow bus queue and glanced at the paper in my hand. According to the very detailed notes I'd written back at my desk in Nehalem, I had thirty-three hours until I boarded a train bound for Cardiff via Paddington Station. Thirty-three hours to see the British Museum, Buckingham Palace, the Tower of London and Shakespeare's Globe. To eat bangers and mash, whatever those were. To mind the gap. I jumped back onto the curb as a truck careened past, honking its horn -- to avoid getting killed by the traffic driving on the other side of the road.

Oops. My cheeks flushed as I looked down, now seeing the bold letters painted on the street directing me to LOOK RIGHT. Oh well, at least I wasn't the first tourist to make that mistake. I crossed the street with care and boarded the bus headed into town, practically pressing my nose to the window until the bus stopped three blocks from my hotel.

With thirty-two hours to go, I dropped my one suitcase in the modest hotel room and ran a brush through the tangled mess formerly known as my hair. I tied a charcoal scarf around my neck and raced downstairs into the brisk fall air. Outside, I breathed in the unfamiliar scent of exhaust fumes. It was the first new smell I could remember in a long time, and I fell instantly in love.

The buildings were so tall, the sidewalks so busy. Vendors pushed their carts and big, black taxicabs paused to pick up passengers. The men had serious faces and the women were so glamorous, sashaying in their stylish heels, with big handbags swinging at their sides. People rushed past the storefronts without seeing the take-out restaurants, Internet cafes, and coffee shops. The caffeine trade was thriving here, too. This tiny bit of familiarity was comforting.

With thirty-one hours and forty-five minutes to go, I climbed onto the double-decker bus touting FULL CITY TOUR in block letters. My scarf caught on the door and I tugged until I set it free.

"Welcome, love. Ticket?" the bus driver asked. I fumbled in my purse until my fingers grasped the paper I'd printed out back home. "Excellent. Have a nice one, love." I climbed the spiral staircase to the top of the bus and sat in the open-top. The air was just cool enough that I was glad I'd worn my heavier coat. I tried to listen to the tour guide, but I was too excited to focus. I was riding on a double-decker bus. In London. This was surreal.

My plan was to ride around the city so I could tell Ardis I'd seen it all, but when we pulled up to the British Museum the art called to me. I all but ran down the spiral staircase, thanking the driver as I jumped out of the bus. I caught myself just before I fell face first onto the street.

"Cheers, love," called the bemused driver. I dusted myself off and waved over my shoulder.

"Cheers," I muttered amicably as I checked for damage. All limbs intact. No blood. I wasn't always that lucky. I walked as carefully as my excitement allowed and stopped inside the museum. This place held more art and artifacts than I ever could have imagined. Where to begin?

Thankfully, instinct took over. I headed to the Upper Level. Once there, I stopped at a small case filled with old coins and jewelry. I squinted at the tiny pieces, focusing on each in turn until I came to the simplest one. The silver charm looked like it could have been worn on a necklace. It had the likeness of an eagle in the center, with curving waves making a circle along its borders. The symbol of Odin, Father of the Norse Gods -- I recognized it from my grandmother's stories.

I tugged fondly at the silver hammer I wore at my neck -- a replica of Mjölnir, the hammer of Odin's son Thor. It was my most treasured hand-me-down from Mormor. She'd worn it every day and passed it to me when I graduated from high school. Right before she died. Mormor's charm was about the same size as the one in the case, and it was exactly the same shade of silver. The card beside the charm said it was found in Scandinavia and was probably made in the Viking Age.

As I stared at the case, I realized I wasn't alone. If the prickling at the back of my neck hadn't tipped me off to the stranger's presence, the positively massive shadow darkening the case would have done the trick. In the seconds it took to pivot on the heel of my favorite black riding boot, I was nearly suffocated by waves of intensity rolling off a figure that fit right in with the Viking display.

My eye-level hit at his chest, where a dark sweater barely concealed the muscles of a well-defined torso. His thumbs rested casually in his pockets and his arms strained against the sweater. I looked up, and up some more, until I finally reached his face. He stood a whole head above even the tallest visitor in the museum, and I'm ashamed to admit my jaw opened just a little as I took in his features.

A shock of tousled, blonde hair rested atop an exquisitely-sculpted face. He had eyes as blue as a cloudless sky, cheekbones as chiseled as pictures I'd seen of the Alps, and lips the pale pink of my grandmother's roses. His jaw was square and strong with a hint of stubble, and his nose looked like it was lifted off a Roman statue. It was more beauty than any one person should have.

Heaven almighty, was this guy for real?

Although Mormor had done her darndest to raise a lady, right now I was entertaining some very unladylike thoughts. I struggled to mind myself, determined to do her proud. She wouldn't have fallen apart at this gooey feeling of familiarity. In my hormone-addled state, I could swear I knew this guy from somewhere.

Yeah, right. If I'd met him before, I would certainly remember it. I could pretty much guarantee that nothing this attractive had ever come through Oregon.

I waited a whole half-minute so I wouldn't be obvious, disproving Ardis' accusation that patience wasn't my strong suit; then I snuck a quick glance. The stranger stared back at me with a look so intense I wondered if he was trying to read my thoughts. Not that I could have formed any right then. I forced myself to inhale. It would be just like me to meet the man of my dreams and pass out cold before he could ask for my number.

He offered a wry smile, so brilliant even in its offhandedness that I had to remind myself to breathe again. The old Kristia, the one Nehalem had written off as the Village Crazy, would have slunk out of the museum before she could embarrass herself in front of such a hunk. But this was the new me -- the me who'd moved five thousand miles from home to experience adventure for the first time ever. I was determined to see how far this newfound spirit would take me. I lifted my chin and gave him my most winning smile. What did I have to lose? My hand raised in what I hoped was a casual wave, and I managed to squeak out my greeting. "Hi."

The stranger opened his perfect, pale lips as if he were about to speak, then closed them. His eyes dropped to the hollow of my neck, where my necklace rested calmly despite my violent pulse. I touched the old-fashioned hammer self-consciously, feeling its familiar coolness. His eyes dimmed with sadness, then anger. He glared at my necklace, his gaze terrifying in its ferocity. I took a step back.

Suddenly, I was in a forest, sprawled across the dusty earth. My body was overwhelmed with pain and my eyes had trouble focusing. Two men were fighting in the distance. One, dark-haired and wiry, waved his hand. Sparks shot from his open palm. They struck the broad–shouldered, blonde Adonis standing ten feet away, knocking him to the ground. He stood and shook himself, charging at Sparky. His blonde hair was a blur as he leaped on his opponent, fists flying in a frightening display of aggression. He was beating the thinner man senseless; any normal person would be dead by now. But the wiry man just laughed, the crazy sound filling the forest with its cruelty.

Oh crimeney, another vision. My strangest one yet.

When I came to, I eyed the handsome stranger. It was obvious he was the blonde from my hallucination. I knew I should be afraid of him, but I just felt confused. If he'd noticed my quirky outtake, it hadn't done anything to lighten his mood. He turned on one designer heel and faced the exit, his body practically shaking with rage.

"I'm sorry, have I done something to offend you?" I probably should have kept quiet, but this whole interaction was beyond weird. Though I was ready with an apology for whatever wrong I'd committed, the stranger just squared his shoulders and stormed down the hallway.

"Whatever," I muttered to his back. If he wanted to be ill-mannered that was fine by me -- the last thing I needed was some uncouth European guy ruining my museum day. Even if he was beyond gorgeous.

I shook my head. Who cared what some half-baked

Viking thought of me? I brushed off the feeling of being the last pumpkin left in the patch and deliberately turned for the stairs. I'd never have admitted, even to myself, that I was keeping an eye out for the stranger. I admired the original Magna Carta and snuck a glance at T.S. Elliot's poems to his godchildren -- the ones that became the musical *Cats*. I don't know how long I wandered, ogling things I thought I'd only ever see in books, but when my stomach rumbled I knew it was time to go.

With a glance over my shoulder, I stepped back into the brisk London day. The smell of car exhaust snapped me out of my fog. With twenty-eight hours to go, I headed to the busy shop across the way to order my very first fish and chips. I tried not to give the ill-mannered stranger another thought, but he was very hard to forget.

2. CARDIFF

"KRISTIA," A KEENING VOICE beckoned. I sat up from my sleep, turning from side to side to place the voice. My hotel room came with blackout shades, something I'd appreciated when falling asleep. I felt differently now. A long finger crooked at me from the darkness. I couldn't make out the face in the shadows, and I wasn't sure I wanted to.

"Who are you?" My voice sounded shaky, though I was going for a threatening vibe. My acting abilities couldn't have hit the broad side of a barn in full daylight.

"Kristia," the voice repeated, now from behind me.

"What do you want?" I jumped out of bed and inched towards the door. Any bravado was totally manufactured.

"Kristia." Now the voice was in front of the door and the long finger motioned again. Every instinct I had screamed for me to run, but I was frozen in place. I was trapped in a dark room with a lunatic and my legs wouldn't move. Fabulous.

"Leave me alone," I challenged, since running like a shrieking banshee wasn't going to be an option.

The owner of the finger stepped from the shadows into the only sliver of light in the room. He was unnaturally tall, wiry and pale, with dark hair combed back from a handsome face, and bright eyes that glowed in the dim light. Slightly pointed ears and an angular jaw offset high cheekbones. He had a charmingly roguish look that made me want to jump into his arms at the same time that voice in my head was screaming *GET OUT!*

"Who are you?" I asked again. The man tilted his head.

"The real question, Kristia, is who are you?" To my dismay, he halved the distance between us. I fought to step back, but my legs were still locked in place.

"How do you know my name?" And more importantly, how could I get out of this room? My eyes darted between the window and the door. One path led to a three-story fall, the other was blocked by a freakishly-good-looking pervert.

"I know all about you." The perv tilted his head the other way and squinted his glowing eyes until they were slits. "Starting with your little gift." He tapped his head with the bony finger and I froze. "Who are you, really? What are you trying to do to my plan?" His voice was a hiss. His eyes glowed brighter and actual flames shot from their depths.

Thankfully, I seized control over my petrified legs. As

the fire landed at my feet, I hopped back in an inept dance, made all the more awkward by my clumsiness. Flames fanned out and quickly rose to block the man from my view. I heard a maniacal cackle that chilled me to the bone and I closed my eyes in panic. It would be death by fire this time. I wasn't sure I didn't prefer freezing.

When I opened my eyes, again I was grasping at my bed sheets, eyes darting around the darkness until I found my bearings. I was in my hotel room in London, and it was not on fire. I was alone. I consciously slowed my breathing. I was pretty sure what just happened had been a dream, not one of my visions. There was no giant elf-man in my future... was there?

I walked purposefully to the window and ripped open the blackout shades, letting moonlight stream into the room. I didn't get much sleep that night.

****

The next day, I got off the train at Cardiff Central Railway Station and made the short journey to what would be my home for the next year. I stood on the steps of the Student Houses, holding tight to the handle of my powder blue suitcase as I tried to capture this moment in my memory. A year of adventure stood in front of me -- exciting subjects to study, sophisticated students and professors to learn with, and brand new sights to see. Nobody here knew me from Eve. For the first time in my life, my future was a blank page. It was perfect. And beyond scary.

With a deep breath, I stepped across the short cobblestone walkway and into a cheerful courtyard. Lined with silvery-green trees and raised lavender beds, the stone-laid square was anchored by a central fountain. A smiling girl sat at a folding table, distributing keys and welcome packets. This was it.

"Name?" The friendly-looking redhead asked in a clipped British accent, her grey Cardiff t-shirt matching the cobblestones.

"Kristia Tostenson." I smiled to cover my nerves. I'd felt a lot braver when this whole trip was just a pipe dream in a coffee shop back home.

"Oh, Kristia! It's so nice to meet you!" She shook my hand before handing me a packet from the stack on her table. "I'm Emma, we're going to be flatmates." She grinned as she reached for another stack, handing over a manila envelope. From the jingling sound, I assumed my keys were inside. "Go ahead and let yourself in -- we're on the first floor, just over there." She pointed. "Victoria's already home. I'll be there once everybody's checked in."

"Okay. See you inside." I shifted the envelope to my other hand, glad to have met a friendly face already. *Please don't have a vision and ruin this. Please, please, please.* My handicap could ruin my first day faster than Ardis' granny could shoot a squirrel off a fencepost. I just wanted to fit in for once.

"We were thinking of going for curries tonight," Emma called as I headed towards the flat. "Do you want to come?"

"Um, yes. That sounds great. Thanks." I fumbled with the envelope as I pulled my suitcase across the courtyard to Unit 3. I used my new key to open the burgundy door -- it was a pretty contrast to the dark gray of the stone façade. I walked into the small living area where a couch, dining table, and four chairs sat opposite an armoire holding a television. Two reading chairs framed a small table holding a lamp. The kitchen was off the living room, and I could see three small bedrooms and a shared bath branching off from the tiny hallway. It was small, but it was clean and comfortable.

A tall girl wearing tight fitting jeans and a stylish top came out of the bathroom, towel-drying short chestnut hair. "Oh hello," she said in a clipped British accent, more upper crust than Emma's comfortable tenor. "I'm Victoria."

"I'm Kristia." I smiled shyly.

"Oh right, the American." She nodded, motioning for me to follow her down the hall. "This room is left, it has a nice flowerbox outside the window." Pointing across the hall, she said, "I'm in there, and Emma's taken that one."

I looked into the empty room. It looked identical to the other two without the clothes and makeup. I stepped through the door, tugging my suitcase with me. The room was simple. The twin bed hugged the wall to my right, opposite an armoire that would be both dresser and closet. The desk and chair were basic. A box outside the window held purple posies. That could be a problem -- I had what Ardis affectionately called a black thumb.

I didn't have much to unpack, so that job was over quickly. The framed photo of Ardis and me at the Oregon Coast took the place of honor on the desk. Victoria was still drying her hair, so I grabbed the Mythology course book I'd purchased in advance and headed to the living room.

I was well into the stories of the Norse Myths that Mormor told me as a child when Emma came through the door laughing. She seemed like a happy person. Victoria was harder to read, but I had hopes for her.

"Let me just pop in the shower and we can go," Emma called over her shoulder, shedding articles of clothing on her way to the bathroom. Victoria poked her head out of her room.

"Are you ready for dinner?" She asked me. I glanced at her stylish outfit, reading behind her words.

"Uh, almost. I just have to change my… um, my top," I guessed, jumping up so quickly I dropped my book on my toe. By the time I made it to my room, Victoria was spraying perfume on her wrists. I sensed my selection would be very different from hers -- Victoria seemed very trendy, while my wardrobe was classic but functional. Slim jeans and slacks, fitted sweaters, tall boots. Proper cold-weather wear, courtesy of a lifetime in the Pacific Northwest and a grandmother who preached modesty. I rummaged through the armoire for one of my newer sweaters and changed my sneakers to a pair of brown riding boots. As I ran a brush through my wavy, dark-blonde hair,

Victoria appeared with a patterned scarf.

"This will go with your eyes," she said simply.

"Thanks," I mumbled, unsure what to make of my new roommate.

"Oh, Victoria," Emma emerged from the bathroom, freshly showered and running a brush through her hair. "Stop 'helping' her." Her fingers made quotes in the air. "You have all semester to give us makeovers." She rolled her eyes good-naturedly and waved us into her room. "Victoria's a fashion student. As her flatmate, you are officially her pet project, whether you want to be or not. Just accept it. I have."

"Oh, tush Emma. If I needed help with matters of mathematics, I would come to you. You know that. I can't help that my specialty is more... practical than yours." Victoria picked up a pair of earrings lying on Emma's dresser and held them up to her ears.

"Pardon me, but mathematics is highly practical. People use it every day. When was the last time you did math, huh? Actually don't answer that. I don't want to know." Emma earned a 'harrumph' from our well-dressed flatmate, who moved to the armoire. Victoria returned, bearing a flowing top and skinny jeans. Defiance in her eyes, Emma pulled out another top and started to put it on. After a moment, she ruefully held out her hand. The gleam in Victoria's eyes as she handed over her choice made me think this was not the first time they'd played this game, nor would it be the last.

"She's always right about clothes, you know," Emma muttered begrudgingly as she dressed in Victoria's chosen outfit. While I considered the pros and cons of having a live-in stylist, I decided this would be a good thing. If I wanted to blend in, Nehalem's fashions weren't going to do me any favors.

When our outfits had been approved, we locked up the flat and walked to Victoria's little car. Emma appointed herself tour guide. "So the first thing you need to know about Cardiff -- the corner market up… here," she gestured, "has the best biscuits. You Americans call them cookies. They bake them fresh every morning, but the packaged ones they sell on the side have chocolate *and* caramel. Delicious."

"Cookies are biscuits, and these are the best. Got it."

"The laundromat just behind us is less crowded than the one in our building--"

"The cutest boys are always there," Victoria finished.

"Good information." I was warming to my more reserved roommate.

"Two blocks this way is the place we get our hair cut -- it's the best salon for the least money. You want to see Robyn. She's great." Emma was one of those enthusiastic people who managed the fine line between cheerful and annoying.

Victoria was eager to point out her favorite places too -- designer clothing shops that were well beyond my spending limit. Emma winked as she teased our flatmate, "And for the rest of us, the good people of H&M have opened a shop at the north end of town. I think you have them in America?" I nodded in response. "Great clothes, but mostly, I pick up the trendy things there, unlike Victoria here who picks up her odds and ends at Harrods each season." Victoria rolled her eyes at us and I grinned at my new cohort.

My tour continued on the short drive and by the time we parked, I felt like I might actually have my bearings. But when we walked into the restaurant, I was overwhelmed by savory smells that were completely foreign. There hadn't been a lot of new experiences in my life, and I wasn't too sure about this one. The hostess led us to our table where a basket of flat bread was waiting. I poked at it suspiciously. Bread was supposed to be fluffy.

"I'll have what she's having," I pointed to Emma as our waitress took our order. Trying to make sense of the exotic dishes listed as entrees was hopeless. "What are you having?"

"Chicken curry with rice. You'll like it." Her smile was reassuring, but I felt no relief whatsoever until the dish was in front of me and I took a tentative bite. I didn't love it, but I didn't hate it either. It was richer and spicier than I'd been expecting, but still good.

"What about your classes," I asked Victoria, bravely tearing off a piece of the curious bread. "What are you taking this semester?"

"It's not about what I'm *taking*," Victoria emphasized.

"I'm doing an internship for a very important fashion house. If I do well, they might hire me after graduation. And then I'll be on my way to designing my own line. That," she sighed, "is everything I've ever worked for."

"Gosh, that would be incredible." I nibbled at the bread cautiously. It tasted bready enough so I dipped it in the curry.

Emma rolled her eyes. "But until then, Victoria can live quite comfortably working for her family's party-planning business. They're one of the top companies in Wales, and Victoria goes home every other weekend to help out. If we're lucky, she'll take us. Her family has an *amazing* country house. And her mum's roasts are super."

"That's true; my mum is a fabulous cook. So is my sister. The whole family loves to cook, really. Well, my dad grills. I bake -- I'm not much for the regular kind of cooking. Just the sweet stuff."

"Tell me about it. Dinners in our flat are nothing to get excited about." Emma admitted.

"I can cook," I volunteered. "I'm actually pretty good at it."

"Thank God," Victoria breathed. "I'll make desserts."

Emma laughed. "Guess that leaves me to clean up."

Well, that was settled easily enough.

"So you spend a lot of time with your family?" I asked Victoria. I'd barely seen my own parents growing up; the idea seemed foreign.

"Victoria's family does everything together," Emma explained. "It's kind of weird." Victoria rolled her eyes and Emma laughed. "I can't hate her too much, even though she's a beast of a fashion critic."

"Of course, it's still nice to get back to Uni." I liked her word for University. "Everyone needs their space, even fabulous, future fashion designers."

"Future being the key word. When are you going to give my wardrobe a break?"

"Hey, enjoy me now while you can still afford me. That goes for you too, K," Victoria winked and I couldn't help but smile.

We finished our meal and paid the bill. We were walking the short distance to Victoria's car when I saw *him* again. At least, I thought it was him. I stared at the window of the pub across the street, nearly positive I was looking at the blonde from the British Museum. He sat in profile, laughing at the animated gestures of the brown haired guy sitting across from him. He looked relaxed and happy, nothing like the cranky Viking I'd met the day before. The darker-haired guy had one arm slung around a ridiculously hot, blonde girl. Viking's side of the booth was empty. I wondered where his date was.

"Coming Kristia?" Emma and Victoria were shivering at the car.

"Sorry," I hustled to join them. "I thought I saw

somebody I knew."

"Who was it?" Victoria started the car and cranked the heater up to full blast.

"Just some guy I saw in London. But it probably wasn't him. What are the odds, right?"

"Stranger things have happened," Emma shrugged. "Now how about some hot cocoa?"

****

Back in our flat, we said our goodnights and headed to our rooms. I lay in bed listening to the occasional car pass outside my window, too wound-up to sleep. My first day was under my belt, I was making friends, and I hadn't had an unwanted vision since yesterday. This year might just be okay. My mind drifted to the blonde stranger and my stomach flipped. Was he really here in Cardiff? What was he doing in the pub? Obviously, he was having dinner, but what did that mean? Did he go to school here? Would I see him again? I forced myself to stop asking questions. The guy hated me on sight. He obviously had issues. And Cardiff was a huge school -- we'd probably never run into each other. There was no point in barking up that tree.

Eventually, I fell asleep, and it didn't take long for my recurring nightmare to begin. It was different this time. The sun was low in the sky, and the wolf and the snake were moving across a field. I was mercifully absent. As the earth was covered in frost and the light began to dim, a lone figure stood in a field of English lavender. He faced the onslaught without a hint of fear: my devastatingly handsome, ill-behaved, blonde stranger.

3. MYTHOLOGY

I WAS IN A great mood when I slid into a seat near the middle of the lecture hall on Tuesday morning. It was my first day of school. I'd always enjoyed listening to a good professor talk about the subject they'd dedicated their life to. And there was nothing more satisfying than typing perfectly-outlined lecture notes -- roman numerals, proper headings, the whole kit and caboodle.

I was untying my scarf when I felt an uncomfortable prickling sensation at the back of my neck. I looked left and right, but nobody was looking at me. I glanced over my shoulder and saw *him* standing in the doorway of the hall, staring right at me. It was the boorish Viking. The guy I figured I'd never see again, and whose stare was making me wish I'd been right. His eyes never left mine as they morphed from furious to confused to sad. Sad was an improvement over the fury I'd seen in London, but his reaction was still weird. I hadn't done anything to this guy, and here he was again, making me feel like I'd kicked his puppy with a steel-toed boot.

Well, two could play at that game. I met his eyes with my own determined look. I'd come to this school for a fresh start and I wasn't about to let some guy intimidate me.

Students streamed by to take their seats, pausing to stare at the stranger's unnatural beauty. The girls snuck glances at the soft, khaki pants and fitted sweater that failed to conceal his impressive musculature. My unladylike thoughts fluttered against my will.

The boys' looks were more resigned, tinged with barely-concealed envy. But the stranger stood still, staring at me, heartbreaking sorrow lining his features. I self-consciously tugged at the hammer of my necklace. The gesture caught his eye, and as he looked down at my neck, his features hardened in anger, nearly settling into the fury I'd seen in the museum. He stormed to take a seat in the back of the hall, never breaking his glare. I glared back until he looked away. Take that, Viking. I thought I'd put on a pretty good show, but when I turned back to my computer my hands were shaking.

Thankfully, Professor Carnicke took the podium and the hall fell silent as she began her lecture. "Mythology." She wrote on the board as she spoke in a clear voice. "The study of folklores." Professor Carnicke was a graceful woman in her thirties, with shoulder-length hair the color of wet sand. She stood at the front of the room with the poise of a dancer. "Early cultures used myths to make sense of a confusing world, to explain the origin of mankind, and to create a sense of history and belonging. We will be focusing on three primary mythological studies: the Norse, the Greek, and the Eastern. We begin with the Norse.

30

"The Norse mythology begins with a trio of prophets. The Three Sisters were the primary Norns -- seers, if you will -- tasked with predicting the fates of gods and mortals. Urd, Verandi and Skuld lived at the Well of Fate and gave water to the Life Tree, Yggdrasill. They supervised a team of lesser Norns who traveled the realms predicting the fates of humans, elves, and non-titled gods. It was the Three Sisters who predicted the fall of Asgard at the epic battle of Ragnarok.

"Ragnarok was Asgard's final fight. Dark elves, fire giants, and jotuns attacked together and most of the gods were slain, so mankind could prosper. This myth resonates as a common theme in many creation stories."

Despite the rugged stranger glaring in my direction, the lecture was off to a fine start. On the one hand, Professor Carnicke was one of the good teachers who spoke really passionately about what she taught. The kind I took detailed notes from. On the other hand, I didn't need to turn around to know that a very large man was boring angry beams into the back of my head from the last row of the lecture hall. The ninety-minute class seemed to go on forever as I concentrated on the feel of the keyboard under my fingers and the clarity of the professor's voice. I didn't raise my head from my computer screen until I heard Professor Carnicke close her textbook. She walked towards her briefcase and put the book inside.

"That's all for today, ladies and gentlemen. Read ahead fifty pages, and be prepared to discuss the tragedy of Ragnarok when next we meet." The room began to buzz as students made plans for lunch. I glanced at my computer.

The screen was filled with well-organized notes, but I was annoyed that I couldn't recall a word Professor Carnicke had spoken. My mind had been too full of images of an angry, blonde Apollo to process much else.

I packed up my bag, tied my scarf around my neck, and stood to leave. He'd gone before I made it to the back of the room. Shaking my head, I walked into the chilly, Welsh air. The stranger was nowhere to be seen. His anger made no sense. But then, I had no idea how guys operated. I was lost as a goose in a snowstorm in every possible way.

I made my way toward the Student Union to meet Emma.

****

"You must be talking about Ull Myhr. Tall, blonde, super fit. Unbelievably gorgeous," Emma drew out each syllable, nearly salivating over the words. I was telling her about my morning, over a cup of tea.

"That's the one." Ull Myhr. What a name. I'd never met a boy named Ull in Nehalem. Then again, I'd only met about thirty boys close to my age in Nehalem, three of whom were named Mike. Emma sipped at her tea absentmindedly. "You know, I had a course with him last semester. It turned out to be my favorite subject."

"Oh? What subject?"

"Don't recall," she giggled. "He's kind of hard not to notice. But he's a graduate student, and so far as I know, he's leaving at the end of this year. Pity. He's one of Cardiff's high points, as far as I'm concerned. And I'm not alone."

"Right." My attempt at nonchalance fell completely flat.

"Not like it matters though," Emma shook her head. "He doesn't exactly mingle with the undergrads. I've only ever seen him really talking to two people -- a guy and a girl who are just as hot as he is -- but I don't know their names. I've heard they all live together off campus, but that's all I know about Ull Myhr. He's half man, half myth around here. But I wouldn't mind finding out a *lot* more, if you know what I mean." Her giggles made me smile.

"Did he seem, uh, angry, to you?" Or terrifying? Beyond irritating?

"No." Emma was surprised. "If anything he looks almost... amused. It's like this whole university experience is funny to him."

Well, maybe I could chalk his general jerkiness up to a bad week. He obviously wasn't himself.

"Do you want me to make chicken parmesan for dinner tonight?" I changed the subject.

"Ooh, yes. Please. Supper has been so much more enjoyable since you moved in with us. Thanks for taking on so much of the cooking. Victoria's dinners were okay, but we all know baking is her culinary strong suit. And I once burned noodles. Honest."

"I don't mind, really. My grandma and I always cooked together. It makes me feel at home."

"Well, I don't want you to feel like we're taking advantage of you. You're just better at it than we are."

"Not at all. I don't have to clean up, and Victoria makes dessert every night. Hey, we might want to talk about that by the way. I'm going to leave this place considerably larger if she keeps making bread pudding." I patted my stomach.

"No way!" Emma laughed. "I'm not giving up nightly goodies for the sake of your figure. Americans are too obsessed with appearances, anyway. Oh and speaking of appearances, James Percy from across the courtyard asked me about you. He thinks you're really cute."

"Who?"

"James Percy, the tall guy, super polite, with dark hair. Glasses?" Emma's eyes were big. "You haven't noticed him, either? Jeez Kristia, are you even looking at boys?"

Oh, I was looking. Just not at the nice ones who were asking about me.

"Anyway, I told him to just come over and talk to you. He's right cute, you'll really like him." She was obviously pleased with her role as matchmaker.

"Um, super. Thanks, Em." My cheeks were hot. Back home, I was pretty much invisible to guys. If I'd somehow caught this James guy's attention, did that mean Ull Myhr was going to stop glaring long enough to see me that way too? Not that I wanted him to -- a cranky Viking was the last thing I needed to deal with right now.

****

Ull was definitely seeing me, all right. In Mythology a few days later, he sat in the back of the room again, staring at me from the last row. His eyes were less angry today, more resigned. I dodged his gaze as I set up my laptop, resisting the urge to turn around and stick out my tongue. If he was going to give me the evil eye during every class, this was going to be a long semester.

Before the lecture started, an unfamiliar, sandy-haired boy slid into the seat next to me. "You're Kristia, right?" The boy stuck out a hand and offered a friendly smile from thin lips. "I'm Henry. Henry Webster. I live upstairs in the Student Houses."

"Oh, right. Kristia Tostenson. Nice to meet you." We shook hands and I looked over the top of Henry's neatly-combed hair to see Ull's eyes narrow infinitesimally. That was interesting.

"Emma and I have Statistics together. She told me she had a new roommate."

"That's me," I typed the date and sat back in my chair. "So you're a math major like Emma?"

"Hardly," Henry actually looked down his nose. He was a good-looking guy and something told me he knew it. "I study business. I'm planning to go into finance."

"Ahh, got it." I glanced up again. Ull's focused stare had zeroed in on Henry.

"And what do you study Kristia?" Henry booted up his own laptop.

"History of Art," I shifted my gaze back to Henry, trying not to laugh at the "v" forming between Ull's eyes. "But I'm mostly taking general ed. courses while I'm here. I'm an exchange student. I did the bulk of my major classes back home in the States."

"Very well," Henry clicked at his keyboard. He stuck out his tongue when he typed -- it was cute. "Has Emma taken you to Naan Palace yet? It's one of our favorites after study group."

"The Indian restaurant?" What was it with these people and their curries? Didn't England have good old-fashioned Chinese food? Or pizza? "We went my first night here."

"Fabulous, isn't it? Let's all three go sometime. Too bad she's not in this class; she's a great study partner."

I giggled. It sounded like Henry saw Emma as more than a study partner. A glance at Ull showed he had misinterpreted my laughter. His eyes were thin slits now, his hands balled into fists. I forced my features into a coy smile and put my hand on Henry's arm, watching Ull's jaw set. Very interesting indeed. "That sounds fun, Henry. Let's grab dinner sometime." Maybe my voice was a teensy bit loud, but Henry didn't seem to notice. He prattled away, making plans while I snuck another look. Ull glared at me, the muscles of his jaw tensing as he clenched his teeth. I shot him a grin and turned to my computer.

When Professor Carnicke dismissed the class ninety minutes later, my gaze wandered toward Ull's seat. It was empty; he had escaped before the lecture was over. Well that was good -- I didn't want to waste any more energy avoiding his mean looks. Did I?

****

The following Tuesday, I sat in Mythology class, third row, taking my standard copious notes. Henry was absent and I hadn't met any of the other students in class yet, so I had most of the row to myself. All around me, pens scribbled and keyboards clicked as Professor Carnicke waxed poetic about the Norse Gods.

It was easy to get wrapped up in the dramatic stories, the romance, the anguish, when the professor was so into her subject. After only a week, this had become my favorite class -- it certainly wasn't because of the bizarre Ull Myhr who sat in the back making me feel an inexplicable combination of emotions. I genuinely liked both the professor and her subject matter. Like I'd written in my last e-mail to Ardis, I was getting college credit for going to story time. It was a pretty good deal.

"That's it for today folks," came Professor Carnicke's dismissal. "Read through the next seventy pages in your text and start working on an outline for your term papers. I will be available for questions during my office hours this afternoon." I bent my head to rummage through my bag as the room began to empty. When I looked up, I spotted the tousled, blonde hair of the student who was occupying far too many of my thoughts. He was looking at me curiously -- the anger finally gone. Well color me pink; that was a nice change. I ducked my head and jumped from my seat, rushing to leave the lecture hall. Once in the hallway, I leaned against the wall and exhaled. When I was sure I could walk, I headed to the quad to find an unusually clear sky. I relished the feel of the sun on my face. I could almost take off my sweater without getting goose bumps. Almost.

I sat under a tree and took out my Mythology book, planning to read ahead for the next lecture. As I turned the page, a deep voice broke my concentration. "May I join you?" I looked up to see *him*. Ull Myhr, who never spoke to anyone, was speaking to me.

"Join me?" I looked around. "Are you serious?"

Ull chuckled, looking pointedly to the ground next to me. "May I?"

"Don't you want to glare at me for a while first? Make me feel like I stole your Granny's favorite baking sheet?"

He sighed. "Please?" It was the first nice thing he'd said to me.

"Uh... um... fine. Have a seat," I gestured feebly,

shock keeping me from standing like etiquette would have dictated. His grin made my stomach flip as he sat next to me, leaning against the tree. I was instantly and immeasurably self-conscious.

"I am sorry, I should introduce myself. I am Ull Myhr. Second Year, Masters in Classics. I did my undergraduate studies at the University of Oslo, Norway. And you are?"

By some miracle I found my voice again. "Um... uh." I had actually forgotten my own name. "I'm, uh, Kristia. Kristia Tostenson. Undergraduate History of Art, visiting student from, the U.S. -- Oregon." I forced a welcoming smile on my face, but it faltered quickly. "Sorry, I'm not trying to be difficult, but this is just weird. Is there something you want?"

Ull looked surprised. "Why is this weird?"

"Um, because you've spent the last week glowering at me? And avoiding me? Why do you suddenly want to talk to me?"

"Kristia, I am sorry if I gave you the impression that I have ill feelings towards you." Ull's sincerity threw me off balance. "Nothing could be further from the truth. I do not even know you."

"I know!" I threw my hands up in frustration. "That's why I'm so confused."

Ull laughed, a hearty laugh that bounced through the trees. It was a wonderful sound. "Well I am sorry I have not been friendlier. This week has been unusually difficult for me. But it is no excuse to have made you uncomfortable." He stuck out his hand. "Can we start over?"

"Do you *want* to start over?"

"I would not have asked if I did not."

"Oh. Okay then." I eyed his hand warily before I shook it. An electric pulse shot through my body, spiking my already overworked heartbeat. It took ten slow breaths to calm my heart. Ull gently pulled his hand back.

"Since we are starting fresh, may I ask you something else?"

"What?" I didn't mean to sound so suspicious.

"Well, my pen gave out mid-lecture. Would you be willing to e-mail me your notes? You type so earnestly, yours must be worth reviewing." Okay, now this conversation made sense. He wanted my notes. I should have been offended he was using me, but he was just so good looking, I couldn't muster up the appropriate level of indignation.

"Oh. I guess." I handed him a pen and he jotted down his e-mail address. Our hands brushed as he handed me the scrap of paper and I pulled back quickly. No point in hyperventilating again before I could tell Emma about this small miracle. The legend himself had given me his e-mail address. I decided to ask him about London -- he may have been having a bad week at Cardiff, but that didn't explain why he'd been so rude at the British Museum. And I was positive this was the same man -- there was no way there were two god-like creatures walking around Britain. If there were, Ardis would have signed up for study abroad years ago.

Study abroad! I kicked myself. I'd totally forgotten the meeting with my advisor. I jumped up so quickly I had to grab onto a tree for support. "Sorry, I have to go. I have an appointment. I'll send my notes this afternoon."

"Of course." Ull stood gracefully, his light jacket straining against defined shoulders. "I would imagine an Oregon girl could use a good cup of coffee. What is your favorite? Soy Latte?"

I shook my head. "Earl Grey. Weird, I know. My dad says he's not sure I'm really from Oregon."

Ull smiled. "Well, I owe you a cup of tea then. It is the least I can do for imposing on your notes."

"And for spending a week glaring at me?"

"I thought we agreed to a fresh start." Blinding teeth peeked from upturned lips. "No fair bringing up my past indiscretions."

"Touché." I caught myself grinning back. This day had taken an unexpected turn.

"I hope a drink will wipe the slate clean. Where will you be at eight o'clock this evening?"

I managed to remember the name of my residence hall. Ull seemed to know it offhand. I scurried off to my meeting, only tripping once on the short walk to the administration building. I could have sworn I heard a low chuckle as I steadied myself, but when I glanced over my shoulder, Ull Myhr was gone.

4. TEA TIME

I SPENT THE REST of the day cleaning. I swept and mopped with manic fervor, then moved on to vacuuming the throw rugs and wiping down every cabinet. When there wasn't a speck of dust left in the flat, I hand-washed all the dishes, then scrubbed the windows with Windex and newspaper until they sparkled, like Mormor had taught me.

By then, I'd run out of things to clean, so I spent an hour obsessing over my outfit, reassuring myself I'd have done the same thing if any other boy was dropping by. This wasn't about Ull -- he'd been so foul all week, I obviously didn't care what he thought of me. I'd just been raised to look my best for company, that was all.

After I'd put on my softest sweater with my favorite pair of skinny jeans and knee-high boots, I bumbled around the living room with even less grace than usual. When the bell rang at eight on the dot I ran, opening the door to reveal the silhouette of a six-foot-five-inch Nordic Adonis. Ull's blue eyes crinkled in the corners and his smile was radiant, a stark contrast to the angry man I'd gotten used to. He wore dark jeans and an ivory sweater that clung to his chest, and his accent was soft when he spoke.

"Hei hei, Kristia. Nice to see you."

"Um... uh..." Oh, come on Tostenson. Find some words. "Uh..." Now! "Yes, it is. I mean, nice to see you too." I could do better than this. I *would* do better. "Thanks for stopping by. You could have just sent an e-card or something." I held the door open inviting him to our small sitting area, and he filled the space.

"I come bearing Earl Grey." He solemnly offered a steaming travel cup. "In thanks for some *extremely* detailed notes."

I blushed. "Right. I've got a little of the compulsive thing. Professor Carnicke is just so enthusiastic; I can't tell what the important parts are, so I type it all. And Ragnarok breaks my heart -- the gods destined to fall so mortals can live in peace. Just awful." I shuddered involuntarily, thinking of Ull's mysterious presence in my recurring Ragnarok nightmare. I wondered what our professor would have made of that.

"Indeed," Ull murmured absently and I blushed again. I was boring him. His other dates must be much more interesting. Not that this was a date. I did *not* want to get involved with someone this moody. No, this was a business deal: tea for notes. And maybe the start of a friendship? Probably not. I usually stuck with friends who were a lot easier to read.

"So Kristia," he began as he sat on our couch, dwarfing it under his lofty form. "What do you think of Cardiff so far? What else are you taking?"

He wanted to make small talk? I could handle that. I'd spent way too many afternoons with prattling old ladies at my grandma's Bridge Club -- I was an expert at small talk. I sat in the chair across from him and dutifully described my archaeology class, all the while looking for a polite way to bring up what was really on my mind.

Since there was no gracious way to do it, I jumped in with both feet. I tilted my face up to stare into his amazing eyes and found I couldn't quite open my mouth. Come on Tostenson. I'd gotten on my first airplane and traveled thousands of miles from home. I'd even stood up to Ull when I'd wanted to crawl under a desk and cry. I could do this.

"Actually," I smiled brightly. "I saw you last week. In London."

Ull froze.

"It's a shame we didn't get a chance to talk then," I tried to look morose as I studied him carefully. "It would have been nice to have a friend coming into school."

A rueful smile spread across Ull's features and he avoided my question.

"You were in London? How did you end up there?"

"My flight from Oregon landed there, so I spent a day sightseeing."

"That must have been enjoyable."

"It was." He still hadn't answered me. I stared, waiting. He didn't blink. "So what were you doing in London, anyway?"

He shook his head. "Sorry. You must be thinking of someone else. I was not in London last week."

Oh sure, there were two, hugely frustrating, Nordic supermodels walking around London. "Liar," I muttered under my breath.

"What was that?" Ull looked amused again.

"Oh, nothing," I coughed to cover up my indiscretion. "Throat tickle." Mormor would have been mortified at my behavior. She'd never have called someone out to their face. "It's just, I've never met anyone quite like you before, and here I meet two of you in a week." I looked him dead in the eye, but he still didn't blink.

"I do not know what to tell you, Kristia," he said gently. We stared at each other for a long minute, each willing the other to back down. Ull won.

"Well, I must've been mistaken." I smiled the too-big smile I get when I lie. I knew I'd get the truth out of him eventually. No sense running him off before I could finish my tea.

"Tell me about yourself, Kristia. What brought you to

Wales?"

Where to begin? Nothing I'd done in Nehalem could possibly be of interest, but I had to say something. I briefly told him about my hometown, my studies at UPN, and summed up my journey by saying I'd wanted an adventure before I settled back into to the life I'd always known.

"I think a life you have always known, a simple life, sounds wonderful," Ull sounded almost wistful.

"It is, in a lot of ways." I wondered why I was opening up to someone who had spent so much energy antagonizing me. "But just once, I wanted to do something different. So here I am."

"How do you like it so far?"

"Aside from grad students taking advantage of my undiagnosed OCD, it's been a pretty good week."

Ull laughed, a musical sound that stopped my heart. It was beautiful and I wanted to hear it again. "I suppose I am taking advantage. One cup of Earl Grey just doesn't seem a fair trade for such *highly* detailed notes." He was teasing me. Ull was in my flat, teasing me. Boys did that when they liked you, right? I couldn't figure this guy out. Ull paused, seeming to make a decision. "Will you let me show you around town this Friday? My classes get out at three, and I can be here at four. The grand tour of Cardiff for your notes. Fair trade?"

This could not be happening. He'd spent a week being unbelievably ornery and now he wanted to take me out?

"I don't know." I kept my face guarded. "Which Ull is going to pick me up on Friday? The nice one from tonight, or the mean one from last week? Because no offense, but I'd really rather not be alone with the mean one."

"Touché." Ull had the decency to look abashed. "You will not let me get away with much, will you, Miss Tostenson?"

"I hope not." I wasn't sure who I was trying to be firm with.

"Well, the nice Ull would like to go out with you. What do you say?"

I wasn't entirely sure. On the one hand Ull Myhr, unquestionably the most desirable student at Cardiff and hands down the most interesting guy I'd met here, was asking me on a date. On the other, the boorish Viking who'd spent a week pushing my last nerve was asking for time alone with me. My voice wavered. "I guess that could be fun."

"Try not to sound too excited."

"Sorry. I'm just not sure what to make of you yet."

"Fair enough." Ull stood, stretching his impossibly long legs. "But you are willing to give me a chance?" I nodded. "Then I shall be here at four." He reached down to pick up his cup. Taking another sip, he eyed me speculatively. His look was so intense it gave me goose bumps and I was glad my sweater covered my arms. He took my hand in his and bent to kiss it with perfect, pale lips.

I stood frozen to the spot as he rose. Piercing blue eyes bored into mine as he whispered, "I will see you Friday night." He strode from the room and let himself out the front door -- good idea, since I couldn't move. My feet were firmly rooted to the same patch of floor, and it was only after I was absolutely sure he had made his way beyond the earshot of our flat that I let out a small squeal. The nerves let themselves out of my body in bursts, and I jumped up and down.

It was this lovely vision that greeted Emma and Victoria when they came home, bringing their animated chatter to an abrupt halt. Victoria raised one elegant eyebrow in question, and my words came in gasps. "Ull. Myhr. Asked. Me. Out!"

Two more bodies joined in my happy dance, and we jumped around the sitting area like the schoolgirls that we were, until we fell laughing onto the various seats. It was Emma who sat up first, asking solemnly, "What are you going to wear?"

****

Within an hour, we had ransacked our collective closets and come up with what we hoped was suitable attire for a date with the most eligible and most confusing bachelor on campus. It hadn't been easy. None of us knew much about Ull, and since we'd never seen him go out with anyone, we had no idea what he liked. Emma offered her favorite dress, a summery eyelet with a pastel sash, but Victoria nixed it with authority. "Too innocent."

"Well, we don't want him to think she's easy!" Emma's retort was in line with my way of thinking, but Victoria shook her head knowingly.

"We don't want him to think she's too *anything*. Trust me ladies, a first date outfit must be ambiguous. It can't say too much. It should be sexy, but not overt – classy, but not boring. Sweet, but not too innocent." She rolled her eyes at our obvious naïveté. "You have to leave him guessing, wanting to learn more. That way, he'll have to take you out again." Emma and I had to throw in the towel. Victoria clearly knew way more than we did about this sort of thing.

Without us to sidetrack her vision, Victoria quickly paired a lace -- not eyelet -- A-line dress, tight in the bodice and flaring to just above the knee, with simple flats for walking. A scarf completed the look, and we added a tailored coat in case the evening was chilly. I had to admit, it looked pretty sharp. I hoped it was worthy of Cardiff's Most Desirable Catch. And he was certainly that, even if his mood swings were considerably off-putting.

I really hoped Cranky Ull stayed home. This was already scary enough.

****

When Friday came, I was literally bouncing with nerves.

I still wasn't positive this was a good idea. What if Mean Ull came back and my date headed south faster than a migratory flock in winter? On the other hand, what if Nice Ull was the real deal? The first guy in... well, *ever* who wasn't trying to get something out of me.

My dating experience wasn't extensive, but the handful of guys I'd been out with in Nehalem had all wanted something. Some wanted to find out what was wrong with Crazy Kristia; some had heard rumors about my visions and wanted me to tell their futures or predict the winning lotto numbers -- like I had any control over what I saw. The rest just wanted to try to get on base.

Ull seemed like someone who had everything -- looks, money, brains. He didn't know about my mental problem, so it's not like he wanted to exploit that. And there was no shortage of girls around here who would have been more than happy to give him an all-access pass. There was nothing he could possibly want out of me -- except maybe my fabulous notes -- that he couldn't go out and get for himself. Maybe, just maybe, he really did like *me*, not my quirky gift, or the way I filled out my jeans. It was my best asset, according to a highly inappropriate comment Ardis overhead at a football game and was kind enough to repeat to me. Starting fresh and winning people over just by being myself... wasn't that what I'd been looking for when I came to Wales?

"Just relax," Emma soothed as she dusted gold eye shadow onto my lids. "He asked you out. I don't think he's ever asked anyone out here. He must be into you."

"I doubt that," I mumbled. "He probably just feels

guilty for borrowing my notes." Either way, I'd been so anxious that I hadn't been able to eat all day.

"Tush," came Victoria's pert reply. She peeked from around the back of my head, where she was wielding a large-barreled curling iron through my thick mane. "Men don't do anything they don't want to do. He clearly wants to spend this evening with you. And why wouldn't he? By the time we're done with you, you'll be the most beautiful girl on campus." Her eyes set in steely determination as she curled and sprayed, creating the perfectly tousled waves I'd seen in her latest fashion magazine. When she was finished, Emma slicked gloss on my lips and handed me the tube.

"Reapply every hour, as needed. Or whenever you're done snogging!" She giggled, and I ducked my head. If only I could be so lucky!

I stood in front of the full-length mirror under the critical gazes of my flatmates. Victoria ran her fingers along the base of my hair, lifting it for good measure before administering one final spritz of hairspray. "Absolutely beautiful," she assessed.

"Stunning." Emma nodded her assent. "He won't know what hit him."

As I looked at the stranger in the mirror, even I had to admit the girls did good work. I was definitely looking, if not feeling, my best. My stomach churned in anticipation. Victoria and Emma let themselves out, heading to the ice cream shop around the corner to give me some privacy when my date arrived.

"We'll see you when you get home… if you make it home!" Victoria trilled over her shoulder as she closed the door behind her. "I wouldn't come home." I heard her mutter as she walked away.

"Me neither," came Emma's muffled reply through the door.

5. FIRST DATE

AT FOUR O'CLOCK ON the dot, there was an authoritative knock. I took a deep breath and picked up my purse. My intuition told me this was a very important moment. I waited for the inevitable blackout to embarrass me, but it didn't come. For once my brain was functioning on all cylinders -- I was vision free. Hey, even a blind squirrel finds an acorn now and then.

When I opened the door, Ull's glorious figure stood on the other side. His thick, blonde hair was in disarray from the Welsh wind. His perfectly-shined boots were the same black as his tight-fitting sweater, and defined forearms peeked out from pushed-up sleeves. The dark wash of his jeans highlighted the long, muscular shape of his legs. He raked a hand through his hair, brushing a piece away from his eyes, and lit up the entire flat with his radiant smile. My heart ached; no man could be so beautiful. I smiled shyly and Ull reached out a hand to kiss one of mine. The touch of his lips on my fingers made me jump, shockwaves radiating all the way down to my toes.

He guided me over the threshold and into the late afternoon sun with one hand on the small of my back. "Are you ready for the grand tour of Cardiff?" I nodded, not quite able to speak. We walked to the street where a shiny, black Range Rover waited, bearing the license plate NORSE1. Of course. He held my hand as I climbed into the passenger seat and my stomach flipped when I realized he was checking me out. I made a mental note to thank Emma and Victoria for their hard work on my appearance.

"Kristia," he said after he had fastened his seat belt. "You look delightful this evening. Absolutely angelic." He raised his eyebrows. "Are you sure you want to spend time with a rogue like me?" Beneath his smile was a serious undertone.

"There's no place I'd rather be." I crossed my feet at the ankles the way my grandmother had taught me and snuck a glance to see how Ull responded to my words. His grimace was the last dark look I saw that night. He seemed to have made a decision, though I couldn't guess at what it was.

He looked at my dress with a wry chuckle. "So I guess ice skating is out." I panicked, trying to remember if he'd mentioned wanting to do something sporty.

"We can go back -- I can change, it's--" his laughter stopped me.

"I was teasing you, Kristia. We can skate another time. I would much rather you wear that dress." His smolder left a warm tingling in my stomach. He reached out to hold my hand and the tingling burst into flames. Desperately hoping he couldn't hear my pulse, I took slow, deep breaths. We were two minutes into this date. I didn't want to give him any reason to go back to avoiding me.

"Right. Another time," I said lightly. Another date with Ull. I had to start the deep breathing all over again. Two and a half minutes into this and I was two for two on hyperventilation. I'd have to start pacing myself. After all, I still wasn't completely convinced that Nice Ull was the real thing. And there was no point in going all ga-ga over someone who might not even exist.

Ull drove toward the center of town, at ease in the driver's seat. I tried to focus on his words as he pointed out Cardiff's considerable highlights, but I found myself lost in the commanding tenor of his voice. I forced myself to really look at the sights, and by the time Ull pulled up in front of Cardiff Castle, I was finally able to hear him. He didn't move to get out of the car, so I re-crossed my ankles and stared at the ancient fortress from the passenger's seat.

"Cardiff has the highest concentration of castles in the world. This one dates back two thousand years, though of course it has undergone many revisions. You just missed the Medieval Mêlée. People dress in costumes; there are sword-fighting contests on the green, turkey legs, and silly games. I went as a jester this year."

I tried to picture Ull Myhr dressed as a clown, but came up short.

"It is nice to walk the castle wall," he went on. "You can see the niches in the stone where guards used to keep their fires on cold nights. We can do that another time --

too late today. The castle closes at six." As fascinating as the wall sounded, the only thing I took from this was that Ull wanted to go out again. Score one, Tostenson.

Ull eased into traffic and his excitement grew as he pointed out Millennium Stadium. His eyes shone as he described some of his favorite matches -- he was both a football and rugby regular, and he glanced wistfully at the stadium when he spoke. It was weird to imagine him doing something so ordinary as watching sports. Maybe he did have a normal side.

Ull glanced at the clock and drove purposefully toward our next destination. The sun was low in the sky as he gestured towards the docks that had made Cardiff a major port for coal transport in the 19th Century, and pointed in the direction of the Arcade, a collection of shops varying from couture to cafes. Naturally, Starbucks was well represented here, too. My head started to spin from the light pressure of Ull's hand on mine, so I resumed my deep breathing to keep myself in check. If this kept up, I was going to have to take up yoga. Yogis were good deep breathers, weren't they?

Finally, Ull turned off the main road and parked in a small lot. Without a word, he got out of the car and opened and closed the trunk. I wasn't sure if I was supposed to get out too -- were we going for a walk or was he just checking on something back there? But it felt weird to ask, so after a minute, I unbuckled my seatbelt and swung open my door.

"Ouch!" Ull dropped whatever he was carrying and rubbed his arm.

"Sorry, sorry! I didn't realize you were there!" This was beyond mortifying.

"Guess I did not open your door fast enough," Ull joked as he stooped to pick up the blanket and basket I'd knocked out of his arms.

"My door? Oh." He'd wanted to open my car door. Like in a movie. How had I made it twenty years and not realized guys actually did that? "Oh Ull." I grabbed his red forearm. "I really got you."

"All in the line of duty." He took my hand. "This way, my lady."

We stopped at the top of the small knoll. The garden easily stretched the length of two football fields, pink, yellow, and purple flowers layering the ground with their thick carpet. Trees swathed in fuchsia petals swayed softly, and a lush covering of grass wove in and out of the flowers. In the distance, a white-columned memorial evoked images of Ancient Greece. It was spectacular.

"Where are we?"

"Alexandra Gardens. Named for Alexandra of Denmark, who became the longest running Welsh Princess." Ull glanced at me from under thick lashes. "This is one of my favorite places in Cardiff."

Ull led me down the knoll and laid the blanket on a grassy spot beneath one of the fuchsia trees. He opened the picnic basket and I wanted to ask him a million questions. He beat me to it as he handed me a bottle of sparkling water.

"Are you enjoying the city so far?" He opened an assortment of tapas for my perusal and helped himself to an olive before leaning back on one elbow.

"Yes." I looked down to give myself time to think of something to say. That beautiful form stretched across the blanket had emptied my mind of all coherent thought. "It's so much cleaner than I'd imagined." Cleaner? I struggled to recover. "I mean, London was beautiful too, but everything was so grey -- grime on the buildings, you know? That was neat, and all, because it was London. But everything here is... uh... *white*." I gestured to the memorial, pristine in its place of honor. "Even the sidewalks seem white. I guess I just expected everything to be dirty because it's so big, but Cardiff's even cleaner than Nehalem was -- and with only three hundred people, it doesn't get very dirty. Well, it gets dirty because it's in the forest. You know, with dirt. And stuff. But not because of litter or anything." I willed myself to stop talking and picked up a slice of bread to end my prattling.

It was a testament to Ull's chivalry that he moved on without comment. "Tell me about Nehalem. What do you miss the most?" He leaned forward on his elbow, seemingly wanting to know.

"Oh gosh." I wasn't sure where to begin. When I was positive I wasn't going to start in on another babble, I told him about my own favorite place. "Well, there's this quiet spot off the main river. If you didn't know it was there, you might never find it. My best friend Ardis and I spent a lot of time there and after she left for college in New York, I used to go by myself to read. Being there made it seem like she wasn't so far away."

"What about your parents?"

"What about them?" I countered before I could catch myself.

Ull had enough manners to keep quiet.

"My grandmother raised me -- Mormor was my mom's mom. My parents traveled a lot for their antique business. They were always on the lookout for new treasures for the shop." I tried to keep my voice neutral. "They didn't want a kid around to slow them down. So they passed me off to Mormor -- she knew me way better than they ever did anyway. She taught me to tie my shoes, to bake cookies, to write thank you notes. Everything I know." I stared at my folded hands. "She's gone now; she passed away right after I started college."

"You miss her." It wasn't a question.

"Terribly."

Ull offered me a container with turkey, cheese, and crackers and as I made my little sandwich, he kept up his stream of questions.

"What are your favorite books?"

"Um…" I chewed, appreciating the change of subject. "I like Shakespeare."

"Romeo and Juliet?" Ull chuckled.

"Much Ado About Nothing." I blushed. "I always saw myself as an un-bitter Beatrice."

"How so?"

"She's so disillusioned with love and doesn't think she can count on anyone -- that part's not me at all. But she's really independent and she's always looking out for her impetuous cousin. It's sort of like Ardis and me. She'd always get herself into these situations because of her heart, and I would come along and clean up after her."

"Sounds tough."

"Not really. Ardis got into the scrapes; I just had to help her out of them." I'd been as busy as a stump-tailed horse in fly time, the way Ardis found trouble. "My part was much easier."

"Always a little outside of life, Miss Tostenson?"

"I guess," I blushed. It was easier to watch Ardis go through heartbreaks than to get hurt myself. But Ull didn't need to know that.

"I know the feeling." Ull's response was wry. "Favorite movies?" He continued before I could ask what he meant.

"Um... Much Ado, again. Kenneth Branagh's pretty fantastic."

"Agreed."

Ull continued as the sun set. He asked about my favorite foods, the music I listened to, and what I hoped to do after graduation. He listened patiently as I told him my dream of working in a museum, and leaned in as I talked about my favorite works of art. He seemed genuinely interested in the minor details of my life, and I told him a bit about the oddities of a small-town upbringing. Naturally, I omitted talk of my little mental tic -- every dog had a few fleas, and mine were bound to show themselves soon enough.

By the time the sun dipped at the horizon, our picnic was mostly gone, and Ull offered me a container of brownies. He held up his sparkling water and clinked his bottle to mine.

"Skål," he said. "Cheers. To new beginnings." He winked at me with a smile so dazzling, I shivered. "Are you cold?" His concern was sweet.

I shook my head. "Everything is wonderful. I'm just... I'm a little overwhelmed. You're --" I stumbled over the words, ducking behind my hair. "You're kind of great when you're being nice."

"Be careful, Kristia Tostenson." He brushed my hair behind my ear, trailing one finger along the curve of my neck. I resumed my deep, calming breaths in earnest. "You could choose much better company than me." There was a warning behind his easy smile.

"I'm not sure I could," I whispered into my water. Ull stared, deep in thought.

"I am afraid, neither could I," he confessed. We watched the horizon in silence as the sky turned from blue to orange to purple. As dusk settled over the garden, Ull packed up the remnants of our picnic and held out a hand to help me up. "To the next stop on our Grand Circle Tour."

When Ull pulled up to the posh nightclub, a new kind of panic swept over me. I wasn't graceful sitting still and dancing was definitely not my forte. But as he seemed to be with everything else, Ull was a natural, leading me around the club as if I'd been dancing all my life. This required that he hold me very close, and the contact was almost too much for my overworked brain. I felt so light-headed that I nearly fell on several occasions. If he noticed, Ull was gentlemanly enough not to say anything.

We left the nightclub much too soon, Ull's fingers twined through mine. I felt a twinge of sadness as I realized our date must be nearing its end. But when Ull helped me into his car, he treated me to another dazzling smile.

"Would you care to join me for a drink at my local?"

"Maybe. What's a local?"

"Ah, Americans," Ull chuckled. "Your local is your favorite pub. Mine happens to be around the corner from your flat. Shall we go together?"

"Yes, please."

Minutes later, we sat in the dimly-lit, wood-paneled room in the quiet pub. We were tucked away in a corner booth opposite the roaring fire. Ull had slid into the seat next to me rather than across from me. His arm rested around my shoulders, so I had no choice but to lean into him in the small space. As we sipped our drinks -- tea for me, an Irish Coffee for Ull -- I finally got to ask him about himself. He spoke unreservedly about his home, winter days spent skiing and snowshoeing with friends, and summer afternoons swimming in the ocean and grilling out at night.

"What about your family? Do you have brothers and sisters?" He'd been so busy with his interrogation I'd stored up what felt like a thousand questions.

"Not so much," he smiled lightly, though I felt his arm tense around me. "I do have a rather sizeable extended family though, makes up for it."

"Are they in Norway?"

"Yes. They all live in the same village actually, but it is pretty remote. Not a lot of contact with the rest of the world."

"How do they feel about you being so far from home?" An innocent enough subject, but Ull's knuckles whitened around his glass before he released his hand.

"They support me as much as they can in my choices, but they do not particularly understand why I would want a life outside of... outside of our village."

At that moment, my mental problem reared its ugly head. Clearly, the night was going too well.

I was sitting in a meadow, underneath what looked like a willow tree. A warm breeze blew its leaves and I looked up at the strange tinkling sound -- the leaves were actually made of silver. At the bottom of the knoll, two swans paddled across a pristine pond. A majestic castle rose as if from the clouds, pink and orange in the setting sun. But it wasn't the setting that took my breath away -- it was the striking blonde man sitting next to me, looking at me like I was the only woman in the world. It was Ull.

It was the first vision I'd ever wanted to stay in. I brought myself back against my will.

"Must be a really nice village." I hoped he hadn't noticed me slip away. Mormor had always told me my little spells were too short for anyone to pay them any mind, but I was fairly positive she'd only said that so I wouldn't be any more self-conscious than I already was.

Ardis had said pretty much the same thing when I asked her. "I dunno, about ten seconds? They're not a big deal, Kristia, seriously. You just kind of get quiet, like you're thinking about something serious. Then you're back to normal again." But she'd had to say that -- your best friend probably wouldn't tell you if you were zoning out like a weirdo for minutes at a time. Still, I hoped there was a grain of truth to Mormor and Ardis' kindness. Maybe Ull wouldn't pick up on my mind trips.

"My village is nice. And my family rarely leaves it. But me." He shrugged, oblivious to my mental jaunt. "I just wanted something different, I suppose."

"And what do you want, Ull?" I glanced up, relieved I'd stayed under the radar. A slow smile spread across his face.

"I do not think anyone has ever asked me that." He thought for a long moment. "I just want to be free to do the things I love -- ski, skate, play hockey. Travel. I spent a winter skiing in the Alps, and it was paradise. It was the only time I have ever felt untouchable -- flying down hills, completely cut off from everything but the mountain. No emotions, no expectations. No pressure."

When he looked at me there was gratitude in his eyes. "You have no idea how wonderful it is to open up to you. I am not able to talk with many people."

"That's your choice -- girls try to talk to you all the time."

Ull laughed. "Let me rephrase. I am not comfortable talking with many people. But you, Kristia..." His look made me catch my breath. "You are easy to be with. You do not let me get away with anything. I can be myself with you."

We sat in peaceful silence, and I listened to the sound of Ull's breathing. I inhaled the woodsy smell coming from his neck, a musky combination of pine and earth. For the first time in my life, I felt like I might actually be where I was meant to be. I wasn't sure if I should be excited or terrified.

But I didn't get to make up my mind. Even pubs have closing times, and with a cheery wave our waitress informed us that time had come. "Well, Miss Tostenson," Ull said with a wink. "I suppose I had better get you home."

"I had a great night," I said honestly. Stupid closing time.

"I did too." He looked into my eyes like he was searching for something. With a sigh, he started the too-short drive back to my flat. He walked me to my door, took my hands gently between both of his, and bent, kissing each hand in turn.

"Thank you Kristia, for the most enjoyable evening I have ever had." My heart thudded with such fervor, I was sure it would give me away. His eyes looked almost wistful as he raised one finger to touch my cheek. I wanted to stand right there forever.

His hand lingered at my neck, and with a whispered "God natt," he walked back to his car and drove off into the cool night. I shivered, pulled my arms around my chest, and let myself into the apartment. I had a feeling my life was about to change in a big way.

****

"Two dates in one weekend. You don't waste time. Where did you say he's taking you tonight?" It was Sunday afternoon, and Victoria was examining the contents of my armoire with a critical eye.

"The castle."

"Lucky wench." Emma padded in and curled up on my bed. "Another date with Ull."

"I thought the castle closed at six."

"It does. But I guess there's some dinner thing they do after?"

"The Welsh Banquet." Emma's eyes were big. "That's fancy. Step it up, Vic."

"Which of these is your sexiest dress?" Victoria stared at her options, obviously dissatisfied.

"Um, the teal one. On the right with the dresses--" I started.

"Between the green dress and the black dress. You color coded your closet?" Emma snickered.

"This is your sexiest dress? This comes to your knees." Victoria's irritation was growing.

"I lived with my grandmother, okay?"

"It's kind of low cut," Emma offered helpfully. "Throw on a push up bra and those four–inch, nude patent heels of Victoria's…"

"My thoughts exactly." Victoria nodded. "Emma, I'm proud of you. You've been listening to me."

"Like I had any choice." Emma stuck out her tongue.

"We'll need major hair. I'm thinking Brigitte Bardot. And a cat eye." Victoria's mind was racing.

"Ooh, can we try that navy eyeliner I got last week?" Emma bounced to her knees.

"With the nude lipstick I picked up yesterday?" I

pointed to the Clinique bag on my dresser. I may have gone out and bought all new makeup when Ull called to ask me out again. Seemed prudent.

"Yes and yes." Victoria clapped her hands together. "Let's get to work, ladies."

****

"Are you sure you will be all right on the stairs?" Ull stood in the grand hall of Cardiff Castle, glancing at the four-inch, shiny death-traps Victoria called shoes. Since Ull's eyes practically bugged out of his face when he picked me up, I had no intention of changing into the emergency flats I'd stuck in my purse. Victoria had scored another hit.

"Probably not. Walk behind me in case I fall?"

"It would be my pleasure."

"On our right, the coats of arms," continued the tour guide. He'd been talking for a good five minutes and I couldn't remember a single word. That's because Ull had started stroking the small of my back when our tour began, and it took all my concentration just to stay upright.

"It's gorgeous." I admired the stonework as we made our way toward the stairs. There I shifted focus to my feet, staring at each step until I'd reached the top. "Made it."

"And I was so hoping I would get to catch you." Ull

came up next to me and took my hand.

"Well, the night is young and these shoes are high. You may still get your chance."

"Tease." Ull kissed my palm.

"Um." I swayed on the heels and he chuckled.

"Come, Miss Tostenson. We are losing the group."

"Right."

We walked the long corridor framed with paintings. It was hard to believe all of the history in these walls. The castle was two thousand years old. The oldest thing we had back in Nehalem was probably the Homestead. Cardiff Castle had about eighteen hundred years on that farm.

"This place is huge," I whispered when we'd caught up to the tour. "I can't imagine living here. How could you ever get comfortable?"

"You get used to it," Ull shrugged. "Find little corners to make your own."

"How on earth could anyone get used to all of this?"

"When you are stuck in it every day it gets old. Trust me."

"Right." Like Ull was an authority on royal dwellings. "Living in a castle sounds *sooo* terrible."

"Depends on the day."

"What does that mean?"

"Just that these walls did more than keep people out --
they kept people in, too."

I thought about my vision from Friday night -- of Ull
and me in a meadow by a castle. Huh.

"Where did you say your family lived, exactly?" I
probed.

But Ull bristled. I'd hit a nerve. "Come Kristia, we have
lost our group again." He took my hand and pulled me
down the hall.

"You may have noticed the Animal Wall in front of the
Castle. Though William Burges designed the Wall in 1866, it
was not constructed until 1890 -- nine years after Burges's
death." The guide lifted an eyebrow as we caught up.
"Please do try to stay with the tour," he admonished before
turning down another corridor. The rest of the group
followed closely.

"Sorry." I ducked my head.

Ull raised a corner of his mouth in a smile. "Why,
Kristia, you are blushing."

"And?" I lifted my chin, and took a step back so I
stood against the wall.

"It is sweet." Ull paused and lifted a finger to my
cheek. My knees buckled and he grabbed my arm to steady
me. My skin burst into flames at his touch. I lost my
bearings again and Ull wrapped both hands around my

waist to stop my fall.

"Sorry," I mouthed. "Must be the shoes." I couldn't stop staring at his eyes. They almost looked nervous.

"Must be." He ran his finger along my jaw, stopping to grasp my chin between his thumb and forefinger. His eyes focused on my mouth and my heartbeat accelerated. He ran his thumb lightly over my lips. They parted under his touch. A wave of heat shot from my lower lip straight to my abdomen. I watched as his eyes slowly moved down then back up, lingering at the neckline of my dress. Victoria had been right about the push-up bra.

"Must be," I repeated.

Ull drew his eyes away from my cleavage and took a step closer. He leaned one forearm against the wall, leaving me enveloped between the cold stone and his warm chest. I was suddenly very dizzy.

"Kristia." He spoke in a whisper.

"Yes?" I whispered back. Ull was looking at me with an intensity I wasn't prepared for. He stepped in, closing the last inch between us.

"Kristia." He spoke again, lifting my chin so my lips were tilted towards his. If his body hadn't been pressed against mine, I would have collapsed in a heap that instant. Instead, I took a shaky breath as Ull dropped his head. He ran his nose along my jaw line, pausing when he reached my ear. He breathed in, the cool air sending a shiver down my neck. With painstaking slowness he drew his nose across my cheek until our lips were almost touching. Now when I looked into his eyes I saw something entirely different. He was strong. Confident. And very much in control.

I let out a small sigh and immediately he covered my mouth with his. It wasn't a gentle kiss -- it was commanding, almost forceful. I melted against him as he claimed my lips, moved down my jaw to consume my neck. My abdomen churned. In that moment I would have done absolutely anything he asked me to.

"Kristia," he whispered again.

"Mmm." It was the best I could muster by way of response.

"I think we need to stop."

In God's name, why?

"Will you be joining the rest of my tour or shall I leave the two of you here?" The guide stood at the end of the corridor, literally tapping his foot. Oops.

Ull placed his hands around my waist to right me. I smoothed my hair and straightened my dress, my cheeks burning the whole time.

"Great timing," I muttered. Just when things were getting good.

"Do not worry Kristia." Ull winked. "We have all the time in the world."

I sure hoped so.

****

"Kristia, oh my sweet Kristia." Great, the keening voice was back. I was shaken from a very pleasant dream, none too willingly, I might add. Thanks to my flat's flimsy curtains, I could see the Elf Man clearly this time. I immediately longed for the cover of darkness. Creepy Elf was sitting in a chair next to my bed, gently stroking my hair. I sat up, incensed, gathered my blankets and held them up to my chin.

"Get your hands off of me! Who let you in here, anyway?" I demanded, feeling a pittance of the pluck I was trying to put off. I ducked as his hand reached out again. "For crying out loud, stop touching me!"

"Let me in? Oh, poor *human*. I can go anywhere I please. Nobody *lets* me in." He hissed through a row of perfect, white teeth. I'd never met anyone who could be both sinister and sexy at the same time. It was disorienting.

"Why are you here?"

"To gloat."

"Excuse me?"

"You no longer threaten me. He will leave. You are not what I feared." His smile stretched from ear to ear.

"What are you talking about?" I inched farther from

him on the bed, trying to get some distance. At the same time, I wanted to reach out for him. I wasn't usually this indecisive.

"Nothing of consequence, sweet Kristia," he seethed. He snapped his fingers and I found myself laying down again, staring up at his glowing face. "But if he comes for you again, if you try to join our world, you will join me instead."

"If who comes for me again? What are you even talking about?" My words fell on deaf, pointy ears. With another snap of his fingers, he was gone. I looked wildly around the room, but there was no trace of Elf Man. This time I was only half sure it hadn't been real.

I tried desperately to go back to my happy place, to the enjoyable dream I'd been having before I was interrupted. I failed. And I didn't get much sleep that night, either.

****

"Oh my gosh! Tell me! What exactly happened at dinner? Don't leave anything out!" It was Monday afternoon and my Archaeology study group had just gotten out. Since I'd gotten home too late to debrief the night before, I stopped by Emma's class with a vanilla latte. Though judging by her pitch, a double shot was the last thing she needed.

"Shh." I sipped my Earl Grey. "What if he hears you?"

"Ull's not in Statistics," Emma sighed. "The only guys we get in there are --"

"Hi Henry," I interrupted loudly. "How was class?"

"Good, good." Henry smiled at Emma as he walked up the path. "What do you think Emma, should we hold study group tomorrow afternoon or tomorrow evening?"

"Evening," Emma voted. "I've got heaps of problems to work through before I could even begin to analyze today's notes."

"Excellent. I'll send the e-mail. See you then."

"See you." Emma waved cheerfully and turned back to me. "So. After dinner. You. Ull. Did you go back to his place?"

"Emma! No! It was our second date!"

"Victoria would have closed the deal in one."

"She would do no such thing," I argued.

"For a guy like Ull? Are you kidding? Anyone would. What's wrong with you?"

"Nothing," I sighed. "Okay, something I guess." A lot of somethings. What *was* wrong with me?

"So, what happened?"

"We ate dinner. That hall is amazing by the way. All wood-paneled and hand-painted and everything."

"Serious?" Emma took another drink of her latte. "I've never been in it. It's not part of the regular tour. It's just for banquets and events."

"Oh."

"Enough about the room. Did he kiss you?"

"Yes." Thinking about it made me dizzy all over again.

"And?" Emma bounced on her toes.

"It was amazing. Everything you'd think a kiss from Ull Myhr would feel like. I literally forgot where I was. And then the tour guide came back all annoyed and Ull said something like 'we have all the time in the world' and--"

"Oh my gosh!"

"I know, right? So after dinner, I figured we'd pick up from there and... we did. Sort of."

"What do you mean 'sort of'?"

"We drove out to this other castle that was built for one of the Marquesses that lived at the first castle."

"Castell Coch," Emma sighed. "So pretty."

"It really is."

"But it closes super early. How'd you get in there?"

"We didn't go in, we just parked on the road and walked into the park."

"But the guards?"

"I wondered the same thing," I shrugged. "But you've met Ull. He's not used to taking no for an answer. Plus the guard was a girl, so that helped."

"Okay, so your date flirted his way into the Castell Coch grounds after hours. What did you do?" Emma tugged at my arm.

"We... well..." I blushed.

"Yes?" she grinned.

"We totally kissed again. It was fantastic. He backed me up against this tree and he just..." What should I say? That he'd grabbed me by the hair and pulled my head back so he could ravage my neck? That I'd had an uncharacteristic moment of indiscretion and let his mouth wander just south of my collar bone for a couple of seconds? That I had been strongly considering asking him to move an inch lower when another guard found us and made us leave?

"And he just what?" Emma was beside herself.

"And he just... kissed me. I can't describe it." I couldn't. Not without turning five shades of red.

"Oh, Kristia," Emma sighed.

"I know. But another guard told us we had to leave, so we got in Ull's car. And he was really sweet and held my hand on the drive home and walked me to the door and everything. But then he just kissed me on the cheek and said good night and that was it. He didn't try to come in. I didn't ask him to." I wasn't a total slut.

"Well." Emma chewed her lip. "Maybe he had an early morning. Or maybe he's a gentleman and he didn't want to steal your virtue."

"He didn't have to steal my virtue." I blushed. "But another couple of kisses would have been okay."

"I'm sure that's coming. When are you going to see him again?"

"I don't know." I shook my head. "He didn't ask me out again."

"He will." Emma finished her drink and tossed it in the trash.

"I hope so." I heard a muffled ringing and dug around in my backpack until I found my phone. I checked the screen. "It's him!"

"You still have a flip phone? Good Lord Kristia, join the twenty-first century." Emma shook her head.

"Hello?" I stuck out my tongue at my iPhone-toting flatmate and answered Ull's call.

"Hei hei Kristia."

"Hi Ull," I breathed. Emma did a poor job of hiding her laughter.

"I like your sweater. That color looks nice with your hair."

I spun around and saw him across the quad. He sat on a bench, his ankle resting on a knee and arms spread out behind him. The epitome of relaxed. A slow smile spread across his face as he stood and pushed a button to end the call. As he walked towards me, my insides turned soft.

"I cannot believe you got to kiss that." Emma followed my stare.

"Shh." I elbowed her in the side. "He might hear you!"

"So?" She rubbed her ribs.

"Kristia." Ull pulled me into a hug once he'd crossed the quad. "What a nice surprise."

"Hi." I tried not to throw myself at him in a desperate attempt to relive the best moment of my life. *All the time in the world, all the time in the world.* "Ull, this is my roommate Emma."

"We had a class together last year. You probably don't remember me--" Emma babbled.

"Emma. How nice to see you again. You study math, correct?"

"Yes. Yes, I do." Emma flipped her hair and stared adoringly. At least I wasn't the only one who forgot their sense around Ull.

"Emma, may I steal your flatmate for a few minutes?"

"Of course." she giggled again. "See you at home, K."

"See you." I waved. I turned to Ull. "Fancy seeing you here."

"My class just let out." Ull jutted his chin towards the humanities building. "But I did not think you had classes on Mondays."

"I don't. Archaeology study group."

"How was that?"

"Fun. I've never taken anything like it, so some of the material is a little over my head. But I'm enjoying it. Professor Copp is a great teacher."

"I've heard good things about her. I think Gunnar took one of her classes."

"Gunnar?" I sipped my tea. Great name.

"My best friend."

"Ah. How'd you guys meet?" I wanted to know everything about Ull.

"We met in primary school. My mom had just married Thor and I was the new kid. Gunnar was the first to be nice to me."

"Your stepdad's named Thor? Like God of Thunder Thor? Who names their kid that?" I shook my head.

"Uh, right." Ull became very interested in his shoe. "Crazy parents, you know."

Immediately I felt dumb. Thor had nothing on Ull in the tough name department. "Sorry, I wasn't thinking. That's probably a really popular name where you're from."

"Yes, very popular," Ull spoke quickly. "There are lots of men named Thor, does not mean they have any relation to *the* Thor. They are just normal men. Not gods at all."

"O-kay." That was a weird reaction. Either something was up or he really did have an early morning. I shifted my tea to my other hand. "So how long did you say you've known Gunnar?"

"About eight hundred years."

"Excuse me?" I paused mid sip.

"You know," Ull tugged at his sweater. "I mean it feels like eight hundred years. Because we live together, and we get on each other's nerves and all."

What was going on? "Are you feeling all right?"

"Yes. Feeling fine. Just tired -- you kept me out late." Ull treated me to a rakish grin and I forgot all about this strange conversation. The only thing I could think about was the way his lips curved up in a smile. And what I wanted those lips to be doing right now.

"I think you could use a cup of coffee. My treat," I offered.

"Thank you Kristia, but I have to meet a professor in five minutes." Ull checked his watch. "May I call you this evening?"

"Any time." I hoped I didn't sound too desperate.

"Excellent." He bent to kiss my cheek. My knees

buckled and he caught me. "We can make plans for this weekend."

"I can't wait." I watched his denim-clad backside make its way across the quad and I hugged myself. The weekend couldn't come fast enough.

6. HEARTBREAK

THE EVENING CAME AND went and I didn't hear from Ull. He didn't show up to Mythology on Tuesday either. At first I was worried. I tried calling him, but his voicemail was turned off -- and I didn't have his home number. I didn't know where he lived, so I couldn't stop by to make sure he was okay. Not that I would have; he didn't need to know how obsessed I'd become.

But a few days passed and I started to think Ull might not be sick at all -- what if he was avoiding me? He knew how to reach me if he wanted to see me again. And my phone was silent. Ugh, I was so naïve. Ull told me what I wanted to hear to get what he wanted. I mean, he'd been a jerk for a whole week, and when he'd needed to borrow my notes, he suddenly got all nice. Then he made out with me in a couple of castles and just disappeared. How did I not see this coming?

The unavoidable truth hit me in full force on Thursday morning. Ull got to know me and he just wasn't that into me. I might not have known a whole lot about dating, but I did know he'd have called by now if he wanted to. There was no way around it. I'd opened myself up to a guy I barely knew and he didn't like me back. Humiliation washed over me in waves.

The problem was that Ull wasn't the kind of guy you could just stop thinking about. Spending time with Nice Ull had been pretty fantastic. And now that I knew how great he could be, how was I going to go back to just ignoring him around campus?

I was going to have to cancel my pity party if I didn't want to flunk out of Cardiff. My first class of the day was Mythology, and it started in less than an hour. "Of course," I moaned, indulging in one last moment of misery.

Mythology. He would be there. I briefly contemplated staying in bed, but the semester was long and I couldn't avoid him forever. It's not like I'd fallen in love or anything. Besides, Mormor hadn't raised me to get all wrapped up in a guy. With a groan, I rolled out of bed and took extra care getting ready.

I used almost all of the products in my new Clinique bag, from tinted moisturizer to lash curling mascara. I even got out the big *and* the small barreled curling irons and teased my hair into the style from the back cover of Victoria's fashion magazine. There was no point in looking as pathetic as I felt.

I tried not to drag my feet as I walked to class, and I slunk into the lecture hall and hid behind my perfectly curled hair. I permitted myself a glance towards his usual seat, but it was empty again. I headed to my row, where Henry was waiting.

"Kristia." He nodded.

"Henry." I nodded back, not having the energy to fake a good mood. Thankfully, he was an easy seatmate.

"You look nice today. Going somewhere after class?"

"Nope. Unless you want to get a cup of tea." I booted up my laptop.

"Rough morning?" Henry typed the date.

"You have no idea."

"Well then, tea's on me." He patted my forearm, a brotherly gesture.

"Thanks, Henry."

"Don't mention it. Hey, do you think you could e-mail me your notes from Tuesday? I accidentally deleted part of the lecture on Jotunheim."

"Sure." I tried not to think about the last guy I'd shared my notes with. Look where that had landed me.

"Good morning, class," Professor Carnicke took the podium, her sandy hair swinging behind her. "Let's begin. On Tuesday we talked about Jotunheim. Asgard had enemies in almost every realm. These enemies worked together to defeat the gods at Ragnarok, but each realm also launched regular attacks on Asgard.

"The gods were divine -- giants, dwarves, and dark elves wanted to see them fall. So Odin developed an intricate series of defenses to preserve his world. Today we're going to discuss the Warriors of Asgard and how they relate to Odin's bloodline. As heirs to the realm, Thor, Sif and their descendants played a vital role in Norse myths."

"Try to pay attention today, Henry," I whispered. "I don't want to have to tell Emma you mooched notes off me all semester."

"Hardee har har."

"Okay. Odin established several lines to defend against Ragnarok. The Valkyries of Valhalla trained the front line. This all-female army rode winged horses to collect fallen, human soldiers from the battlefield. They brought them back to Asgard and taught them to fight for Odin.

"But Odin knew the Valkyries were not enough. While they trained soldiers for Ragnarok, someone had to handle the day-to-day attacks on the realm. The Warriors of Asgard were Odin's preemptive line. They traveled throughout the realms, eliminating threats as they arose. When Odin got word of a Fire Giant uprising, he dispatched his Warriors to Muspelheim. When the Dark Elves found a way to breach Asgard, the Warriors were sent to Svartalfheim to dispose of the conspirators. Odin was unsympathetic and unforgiving -- any threat to Asgard was a capital offense, and the Warriors had orders to kill anyone involved."

"Sounds kind of harsh," I whispered to Henry.

"Not really." He shrugged. "If your death was prophesied, wouldn't you kill first ask questions later?"

Maybe.

"Odin's son, Thor, had a special connection to the Warriors. The God of Thunder used his hammer, Mjölnir, and his belt, Megingjörd, to literally crush his enemies. And he worked closely with the Warriors to train them for battle. That's how he came to meet a warrior named Sif, who also happened to be the Goddess of Beauty. He married her and adopted her son, Ullr." She wrote the name on the board.

Ullr. Just one letter off from Ull. Even when I wasn't thinking about him he managed to creep into my day. Jerk.

"You okay?" Henry shot me a look.

"Sure. Why?"

"You're typing *really* loud. You're going to break your keyboard."

Oops.

"Little is known about Ullr, though based on the number of sites throughout Scandinavia bearing his name, he must have played a vital role in early Norse cultures. It is believed his father was a warrior who died in battle. And on becoming Thor's stepson, Ullr became a titled god -- God of Winter."

What had she just said? I scanned my notes, reading back Professor Carnicke's words. *Thor's stepson, Ullr... God of Winter.* A deity with a stepdad named Thor going by the name of Ullr... or Ull.

It couldn't be possible. Could it?

****

I wasn't going to get an answer any time soon. Ull never did show up to class, and I didn't see him around campus the rest of the day, either. Usually, I caught a glimpse of him getting tea between classes, or heading through the east door of the library in the early afternoon. I didn't know his schedule or anything, but he stood out; it was hard not to notice him.

I did a good job of going through the motions the rest of the week without thinking too much about whether I'd kissed a real life god. I went to classes, smiled at Emma's jokes, even went out for ice cream with my flatmates. By Friday afternoon, I still hadn't seen Ull around campus, and my curiosity got the best of me.

Since pride goeth before the fall of the world's most useless psychic, I decided to swallow what little I had left and call him. The least he could do was tell me that he wasn't into me. I braced myself as I dialed his mobile. One ring, two. I could hang up now and spare myself any more embarrassment. Three rings, four. Oh, right. Stupid caller ID would out me even if I hung up now. Five rings. Then a click, as the call was forwarded to Ull's voicemail.

So he'd turned it on. My palms got all sweaty at the velvety sound of his voice. The outgoing message said he'd gone out of town for a while, and would check his messages periodically. Was the idea of a third date so awful that he'd run away?

"Uh, hi Ull," the short beep caught me off guard. "I just wanted to say, um… hi, since you know, I haven't heard from you… about getting together this weekend." Oh, good heavens. Of course he knew that. "I mean, I'm sure you're busy, and I understand if you, uh, don't want to call." Stop. Talking. NOW. "But you weren't in class, and, well, I, uh, just wanted to make sure you're okay. I mean, I'm sure you're okay. You probably just, um… yeah. Talk to you later." I banged my head against the wall. Thankfully, I'd stopped babbling before I could tell him I really wanted to make out again. I had some dignity.

That night my Ragnarok nightmare came back.

As I stood in a field of English lavender, Ull suddenly appeared at my side. He didn't acknowledge me. His eyes were focused on the horizon, waiting for attack. I was so surprised to see him that I forgot all about the snake and the wolf, who were bent on killing us.

"What, now you decide to show up? Where have you been for the last week? You couldn't pick up the phone to let me know you were okay?"

Ull's eyes flickered towards mine without a hint of remorse. "I was protecting you."

"From what?" I glared at him while the snake wove a path through the purple field.

"From this. All of this," Ull gestured around the field, his eyes coming to rest on the enormous wolf circling us. "You have no idea what you are getting into."

That was all he had to say. Everything turned red. I was so full of anger -- anger at Ull for dumping me, anger at myself for caring. Anger that I was letting some guy take my focus off my amazing European adventure.

"Well thanks a lot Viking, but you know what? I've got this covered." My rage boiled over and I grabbed a sharp stick that was sitting on the ground, clenching it in my fists and looking for something to kill. The snake came first, standing on its tail and bearing its fangs as it prepared to strike. But I was faster, slamming the stick into its body and impaling the creature that'd killed me hundreds of times before. It froze mid-strike, shock on its reptilian features before it fell limp at my feet. Ull took a step back, obviously caught off guard.

"Not so helpless after all, am I, Mr. Perfect?" My hand twitched as the wolf circled slowly, intent on avenging its friend. It was no match for my pent up anger. The rage built again and I charged for the animal, staking its eye and making it cry out. It ran into the darkness, yelping all the way. For the first time ever, I had won. And I'd done it on my own.

When I woke, I felt better -- stronger. I still wished things had worked out differently with Ull, but I was done hoping for a call that wasn't going to come from a guy I barely even knew, who may or may not even be human. I'd come all this way for an adventure. Was I really going to waste my time mooning over some tacky guy who couldn't be bothered to pick up the phone? I didn't think so.

****

The next week came and went and Ull never came back to class. Well, fine. Who needed a tortured Viking anyway? Without Ull around, I was able to relax, smiling through conversations with my new friends and even going for tea again with Henry after Mythology. He only asked me about Emma three times. I made a note to put in a good word for him.

When Friday rolled around, Victoria and Emma came home bubbling with big disco plans. A group of their friends was getting together at a local club and the girls were determined to drag me along.

"Oh, I don't know," I demurred. "I really wanted to watch that marathon of Sports Wives tonight." I gestured to the pizza box in front of me, flanked by two packs of those caramel-chocolate McVities "biscuits" Emma had gotten me hooked on.

"No can do, missy. We know you were down about Ull, though you've been doing a fab job of *keeping calm and carrying on*, as we say." Victoria winked at me.

"I'm not upset about Ull. Seriously," I added when Victoria frowned. "That's last week's news. I really, really want to watch Sports Wives and eat these ridiculously good cookies."

"Sorry, K. Emma promised James that you'll come out with us tonight and he is determined to make a go of it with you."

"Who?"

"James. From across the courtyard. Kristia, we *talked* about him." Emma tapped her foot.

"Oh, right. Where did you say you're going?" I eyed my biscuits with longing.

"Dancing."

"Uh, no." I shook my head. "Not the best activity for me." I lifted my fuzzy slippers. "Two left feet. See?"

"Forget it, Kristia. You're going." Emma was firm. Victoria squared her shoulders.

"Oh, fine. But only if I can wear something of yours."

Victoria's eyes lit up. "I was hoping you'd say that!" She ran off, her eyes glossy as she dove straight into her armoire.

****

I regretted my words as we walked the short distance from the parking garage to the club. Victoria had outfitted me in a teensy dress and stiletto boots. What was she thinking putting me in three-inch heels to dance? Even so, it was nice to be out with the girls.

They were making me laugh with racy stories about their early years at Cardiff, and I was actually excited to meet the guy they were so insistent on setting me up with. But when we walked up to the very same nightclub I'd been to with Ull, my stomach dropped. I may have been done pining, but it didn't mean the rejection didn't still sting.

I told myself I only had to smile for a few hours and then I could crawl into bed. Those biscuits would even still be waiting for me. Head held high and mindful of my step, I followed my giggling girlfriends into the club.

7. THE NIGHTCLUB

BEFORE I TOOK TWO wobbly steps into the nightclub, I knew I'd made a mistake. Coming here with Ull had been amazing -- dancing in his arms, breathing in that smell that seemed too good to be real. The only things I smelled now were stale beer and sweaty frat-boys.

"Come on, love." An over-eager James was waiting inside the club. He wasn't bad looking, if you were into the whole Clark Kent thing. He was tall and dark, with retro glasses that were either extremely dorky or hipster cool -- Victoria could have said for sure.

He tugged at me the minute I'd taken off my coat. "Let's dance!"

I tried; honestly I did. But my mind was on my last dance partner, the way he'd easily led me around the floor as if from another era. Dancing with James wasn't nearly so nice. The caramel McVities waiting for me at home were the only company I wanted.

"Sorry," I mumbled as I backed away. "My shoes, um... hurt." That wasn't exactly a lie. At the bar I ordered a tonic water and slumped on the stool. I had a headache from the flashing lights and runny eyes from a nearby cigarette. My flatmates were at the far end of the room, dancing their hearts out. They wouldn't miss me if I slipped out for a while. I put my drink down and turned to leave.

I hadn't made it far when a belligerent frat-boy type moved into my path. He sloshed his drink, narrowly avoiding my boots. I tried to step around him, but he slid an unwanted arm around my waist. His grip was too tight -- he was stronger than he looked.

"Hey baby. Wanna dance?" It was a command and the group behind him shouted their encouragement. I immediately regretted not checking in with my friends. If I had, maybe someone would have offered to walk me home.

"No thanks." I tried to twist out of the guy's hold, but he grabbed my arm.

"You're not going anywhere." The group closed in around me, pushing me towards the back exit. I looked frantically for Emma and Victoria. Why didn't anybody notice this was happening? Of course, with the flashing lights, we probably looked like a group of friends dancing. I thought about kicking the one holding me -- drunk as he was, I could confuse him, at best. But even if I knocked him down, I'd never get through the whole gang. It didn't matter; I had to do something. I squared my hips, preparing to fight.

"Leave me alone," I yelled, hoping that someone would

hear me over the din. The boys laughed harder. As I psyched myself up to kick the one leeched on my arm, a tall figure stepped from the shadows. His brow was furrowed and his eyes burned with fury. He towered over the crowd as he squared his shoulders. A lock of blonde hair fell over one livid eye, and the growl that came from his throat sent a wave of alarm through the circle. I felt immediate relief. Nobody was going to mess with Ull.

"Is there a problem?" The words were a threat, and some of the fringe members stepped back involuntarily, blending into the crowd.

"Yes!" I cried, just as the boy holding my arm slurred, "Naw, man. We were just going outside." He slung a drunken arm over my shoulder, defying me to disagree.

My towering savior shook his head. "I heard the lady tell you to leave her alone." He took one menacing step into the center of the group, sending all but my attacker scattering. The boy was drunk, but not drunk enough to pick a fight with my enraged hero, and he backed away waving his hands in surrender.

"Hey man, I didn't mean anything by it." He whipped his head back and forth looking for a way out. Ull grabbed him by the collar and lifted him off the ground with one arm. I'd never seen anyone do that in real life. The boy dangled helplessly mid-air. He winced, anticipating the blow.

Ull leaned down to hiss into his ear. "I know exactly what you meant."

"C'mon man, she wanted it." Wrong thing to say. Ull's eyes blazed and his arm started to shake. "Can't. Breathe." The boy choked on the words. Ull's mouth twisted into a half smile and suddenly he and the boy were gone. They literally vanished into thin air. One minute they'd been standing two feet from me, and the next -- poof. They were nowhere to be seen.

"Ull?" I pivoted a full circle. He wasn't there.

"Did you see that?" I turned to the couple next to me but they shook their heads. Had I imagined the whole thing? Was I even crazier than usual?

"Kristia," I heard Ull's voice before I saw him. He was coming through the back door. He crossed to me and pulled me into a hug. "Thank goodness you are all right. That cretin will not bother you again."

Okay, what was going on?

"Where did you go?" My question was muffled by Ull's chest. He was holding me really tight.

"I took the jerk outside, gave him a stern talking to."

"Right," I tried to pull away, but Ull was too strong. "Let go, Ull." He did, reluctantly. "I mean where did you go? You just disappeared like some magic trick."

"I walked outside, Kristia." Ull shook his head.

"No you didn't. You had that guy by the neck and then he said I wanted it and you just --" I twirled my finger. "Poof. Gone."

"It has been a long night. Wait here," Ull commanded, and while I didn't appreciate taking orders, I didn't think to disobey. He had a brief talk with the barman, no doubt making sure the perps couldn't cause any more harm, and came back with our coats on his arm. I didn't ask how he had known which jacket was mine.

"Come Kristia, I am taking you home." He strode across the dance floor, still shaking, as I hastily told my roommates I would meet them at our flat. Outside, it was so cold the trout must have been tap dancing, and Ull's long legs took strides so big I had to run to keep up. He stopped under a streetlight and his breath came out in small puffs. His body was tense, but his eyes were so soft, the grey-blue of the sky after a storm. I both adored and hated him all at once.

"Are you all right, Kristia?" he asked with genuine concern.

"I'm fine, thanks. How did you ..." My sentence trailed off.

He drew another ragged breath. "Right place, right time, I guess," he said halfheartedly. He obviously wasn't telling the whole truth. I scanned his face and he shrugged.

"That's not what I mean. Are you going to tell me about that whole disappearing act in the club?" Or explain how he and his stepdad had the same names as the gods I'd taken a quiz on this week?

"Not tonight."

"Then goodnight, Ull."

"Wait." He seemed at a loss. "I suppose we should talk."

"I don't know if I want to talk to you. You didn't call me, remember?" I sounded a lot more bitter than I meant to.

"Right. That. You deserve an explanation." Ull had the grace to look ashamed, but it only fueled my anger.

"For what? Making out with me in the middle of a castle -- no, two castles -- and just leaving me hanging? For lying to me about having '*the most enjoyable evening you have ever had*' and then not bothering to call when you said you would?" My exaggeration of his soft accent was terrible.

But I was building steam. "It's been two weeks and I've heard nothing from you. Nothing! I actually believed you when you said Nice Ull was the real you. Was that some kind of a joke? Because clearly, you're the same jerk who spent a week giving me nasty looks for absolutely no reason."

"I would hardly say I am a jerk, Kristia."

"Really? Then what would you call making out with someone all night and then dropping off the face of the earth? You made me feel this big." I pinched my fingers together and held them just under his nose. "And where do you get off acting like that? What kind of scumbag just drops the cow once he gets a taste of the milk? Huh?"

"Would you be the cow in that scenario?"

"Don't mess with me right now, buddy," I threatened. "I called you. Because that's what nice people do when the person they like goes missing. They pick up the phone and call. I thought something awful had happened to you. I was so stupid! Was this whole thing just some ploy to see how far you could get with me?" The corner of Ull's mouth turned up in a smirk. It infuriated me. "Oh, so this is funny to you?" I winced a little at the shrillness in my voice. It wasn't dignified, but he had it coming.

"Nobody here has ever spoken to me like this." Now the smirk was a full-fledged smile.

"Well somebody needs to. You think because you're so superior, you can just parade around and do whatever you want? Do the rest of us even matter to you?" I was shaking, my hands balled into tight fists.

"Are you finished?"

"Hardly," I muttered, glaring into Ull's endless blue, traitor eyes.

"I did just save you," Ull reminded me.

"I had things under control." My voice was testy.

"Oh, did you?"

"I was getting there."

"Right. Well, while you were getting there, I took care of the problem. The least you can do is let me explain." I thought about what I'd be doing right now if Ull hadn't come along in the nightclub. Guilt stepped lightly on

Anger's toes.

"You know what Ull?" I sighed, too exhausted to fight anymore. "I've had a long night. I just want to go home."

"Do you want to hear my explanation?"

"Do you think it'll make any difference?"

"Maybe."

I shook my head. "Maybe's not good enough." I turned and walked towards campus.

"Where do you think you are going, Kristia?"

"I told you. Home." Heavy footsteps followed me.

"This conversation is not over." Ull sounded strained.

"Yes, it is. I get it. You weren't that into me. You're lousy at dumping girls. Case closed."

"Kristia," Ull grabbed my hand, forcing me to stop. "Please. It is not what you think."

I pulled my hand back and folded my arms. "It doesn't matter, Ull. I just want to go home." As I started my brisk walk, Ull matched my pace.

"Fine. You may go home."

"Gee, thanks." Could he be any more arrogant?

"But this conversation is not over," He marched confidently beside me.

"Where exactly do you think you're going?"

"With you."

"You are not coming home with me." I didn't care how good he looked in that coat, I was a woman of substance.

"I am making sure you get home safely, whether you like it or not. We can talk tomorrow." The smugness in his voice got under my skin.

"I seriously doubt that," I muttered, picking up my pace in an effort to get away from him. At that moment, Ull was the last person I wanted to be around.

****

"Uh, Kristia." Emma's voice trilled through my bedroom door at an ungodly hour for a Sunday morning. "You have to get out here."

Reluctantly, I grabbed my favorite slippers and tied my ballet sweater around the thin camisole I'd worn to bed. Shuffling towards the hall, I rubbed the sleep from my eyes. "This better be good, Em."

"Oh, it is," Victoria grinned from the couch where she sipped at a cup of coffee. She gestured to an enormous bouquet on the table. White roses filled the room with their heady scent, and hydrangeas and foxgloves filled out the arrangement. "They're for you," Victoria finished.

"Who…" But my insides churned when I opened the card. '*I am sorry. Call me. Ull.*' I crumpled the card and chucked it into the trash bin. Letting out a sound that would have earned Mormor's disapproval, I stomped back to my room. If Ull thought some stupid flowers would make me fall all over him, he had another thing coming.

"Wait! Who are they from?" Emma pleaded.

"Who do you think?" I could almost hear Victoria roll her eyes as I slammed my door. Ull was getting on my last nerve.

****

By the time my next Mythology class rolled around, I'd successfully avoided five of Ull's calls and one personal appearance at my flat, no thanks to the lousy acting skills of sweet Emma, who was highly unconvincing in declaring I wasn't home. I slipped into class at the last possible minute, but Ull was still waiting inside the door.

"Kristia," he greeted me with his impossibly arrogant grin.

"Ull," I acknowledged before making a beeline for the front row. He wouldn't be able to bother me under the professor's nose.

"Kristia," Ull sighed. "We can do this all year. I have nothing but time." He took the seat next to me as I focused on setting up my computer. "But trust me, you want to hear what I have to say."

"I highly doubt that," I muttered with all the civility I could manage. Use me once, shame on you. I wasn't interested in going down that road again. Thankfully, Professor Carnicke chose that moment to launch into her lecture, and for ninety blissful minutes, decorum required Ull's silence. As soon as she closed her book, I jumped up, stuffing my laptop into my bag and tripping over my feet in my rush to leave the room.

"Careful, Miss Tostenson," of course Ull was right there to catch me. I snatched my arm away.

"Listen," I countered angrily. "You aren't into me. I get it. Stop following me around! Just let me be."

"You do not mean that."

"I really do! It's embarrassing enough to have to see you every day, the last thing I want to do is listen to why you don't want to go out with me again. You don't owe me anything. Honest. Please, just leave me alone."

"Kristia, it really is not like that."

"I don't care what it's like. I have to go." I raced out of the classroom and didn't stop until I reached the Student Houses. I threw myself onto the couch and dropped my head into my hands. No wonder I'd always stayed away from guys. My life suddenly felt way too complicated.

****

"Uh, Kristia?" Victoria knocked on my door the next evening.

"Come in." I raised my head from the literature text I was studying. Molière was always good for a laugh. "What's going on?"

"Well, I don't mean to bother you, but I just tried to leave the flat and I was stopped by these." She held up a handful of white orchids. "And there are heaps more where they came from." Her glee was poorly disguised.

"You think this is funny, don't you?"

"You have to admit, most girls would be over the moon if Ull Myhr was sending them flowers."

"Stalking them, more like it."

"Whatever." Victoria shrugged. "I brought the rest into the living room. I'm not one to tell you what to do--" I snorted at her blatant lie. "In matters of the heart," Victoria continued indignantly. "But if the lad is that determined to talk to you, I'd wager he has something pretty important to say."

I rolled my eyes and made my way down the hall. "What the…" Every surface of the living area was covered in vases of white flowers. The scent was simultaneously heavenly and cloying. I picked my way through the arrangements until I found the biggest one. I opened the attached card with a resigned groan.

'Kristia,' it read. *'Please hear me out. I left because my life is complicated, and I do not know if it is fair to involve you. I want to tell you everything, but if you really want nothing more to do with me, tell me in class tomorrow and I will leave you alone. Ull.'*

Oh, crimeney. What was I supposed to do now?

****

The next morning, I hovered outside the classroom with two minutes to spare, still unsure. On the one hand, he'd dropped me once. I wasn't so stupid as to head blindly down that path again, and he was giving me an out -- say the word and he'd leave me alone for good. On the other hand, I really had enjoyed our dates. And no guy had ever worked so hard to win my attention.

Heck, until recently, no guy had ever brought me flowers -- and here Ull was spending the gross national debt on white blooms. A small part of me still held onto the hope that Ull might be the first guy ever who liked me just for me. While a bigger part of me was screaming *'don't be a fool! Run!'*

I shook my head. I had no idea what I was going to do.

I kept my head high as I walked into the room. A quick scan revealed Ull in the third row, seeming relaxed as he leaned back in his seat. But a closer look showed he was gripping his pen and his shoulders were squared. He was waiting for me. And he was nervous. I made up my mind, easing my way into his row and carefully sitting two seats away. Ull turned with a tight smile, cocking his head to one side.

"What does this mean?"

"It means I'm still mad you didn't call. And it means I still don't trust you. But I'm willing to hear you out." I kept my hands balled in my lap. "And thank you for the flowers."

Ull's face lit up. "I am so glad." He exhaled and the tension visibly left his shoulders. "I will pick you up at eight o'clock tonight. We can talk then."

"Tonight? What's wrong with now?"

Ull tilted his head towards the podium where Professor Carnicke was opening her book. "Would not want to be rude, would we?" He gave me an infuriating wink and turned his attention to the lecture.

****

At eight o'clock, a firm knock interrupted my reading. I picked my way through the flower shop that our living room had become and opened the door.

"Oh good, you kept my peace offerings." Ull treated

me to a rakish grin.

"Just a few of them," I muttered. "Come on in."

"Oh, no. You must come with me."

"Why?" I challenged. Ull sighed.

"Are you going to fight me at every turn?"

"Probably."

"Please come." He looked so adorable standing on my stoop, his scarf casually thrown across the grey sweater under his coat. I gave in quicker than I meant to.

"Fine." I grabbed my coat from the closet by the door and shoved my keys and wallet into the pocket. "Where are we off to?" I closed the door behind me and followed Ull into the brisk night, waiting for his promised explanation.

But he didn't say anything. Instead, he put his hand on the small of my back and guided me away from campus. I shivered and noticed that Ull wore his jacket open, at ease in the chill. As we rounded the corner, Ull dropped his hand to clasp mine. It was so warm, so strong, and for a moment I forgot to be mad at him. We walked in silence as he led me down the main road. After two right turns, I found myself standing in a quiet garden. Ull had brought me to a church.

8. THE NORSE CHURCH

"HAVE YOU BEEN HERE before?" Ull's voice was soft. I looked around the courtyard, covered in flowers, with vines trailing up the sides of the charming chapel.

"No," I answered. The square was beautiful, but I'd been promised answers.

"I come here a lot. Sometimes I just walk the garden." Ull sat on a stone bench, somehow even more beautiful in the moonlight. An eternity passed before he started talking.

"This is a Norse Seaman's Church," Ull spoke quietly. "It wasn't built until the mid-twentieth century, but it blends with the town's older buildings." I wrapped my arms around my chest. I wasn't in the mood for another history lesson.

"It's very peaceful." It was all I could think of to say.

"Yes," he said calmly. We stared at the bounty of ivory roses growing in the eastern corner of the garden, and the ivy stretching up the white walls of the chapel. "When I am here I can forget…" His body tensed, his brow furrowed, and his eyes grew dark. I sighed -- Angry Ull.

"Uh, you lost me." But no clarification was forthcoming. I was uncomfortable waiting. It wasn't exactly evening stroll weather.

"So are you going to give me this alleged explanation or not? Taking me to a church doesn't exactly cut it." I glanced impatiently at Ull's tense frame. I didn't know what to make of him. I waited for a response but he kept looking at the sky.

"Seriously Ull? You dragged me out here in the cold for nothing? That's it -- I'm done." I turned to walk away. This was the worst fairytale ending ever.

"Kristia." He hung his head, staring at his hands. I stopped but didn't turn. "Please come sit with me."

"Why?"

"Please."

Curious and desperate for his companionship, I sat. I shivered as a gust of wind blew through the garden. I pulled my coat tighter around me. Ull took off his scarf and wrapped it around my neck. The gesture would have been sweet two weeks ago.

"I owe you an explanation."

"We already established that."

"Kristia, let me talk!" He looked up with pleading eyes. They bored into mine, as if he could see through my pretense and right into my broken heart. He took a deep breath, his broad shoulders rising and falling with effort. He unclasped his hands, then clasped them again until his knuckles turned white. "Kristia, I had a very nice time on our dates. Those days with you were the best I have had in- -" He stared at the ground. "In a long time."

"Right. Then why did you just take off?" The words were out before I could stop them.

Ull thought. "Come with me." He stood. I followed. But I hesitated when he opened the church door.

"Are we supposed to be in there?" Rule followers did not break into churches at night.

Ull laughed. "The pastor is a friend." He ushered me into the warm chapel. Row after row of chocolate-colored pews were stunning in their simplicity. The wood of the benches shone with fresh polish and the little altar at the front of the aisle held a pulpit with a carved crest -- a hammer, a cross, and a figure I didn't recognize. The room was small for a church, and very plainly decorated. Only the woodwork and the crest stood out. It was enchanting.

Ull left me sitting in a pew and came back with a plate of heart shaped waffles with jam, and two cups of tea. I must have looked suspicious because he laughed. "Honest, I am a regular here. It is okay with the pastor. I told him we are in the chapel. He says 'hei hei' and 'god natt'. Hello and good night."

The waffles did look good, and the tea warmed my hands as I took a sip. So long as I wasn't breaking, entering, *and* stealing food from a church, this night could still end well. A begrudging bite of the waffles proved me right. "These are really good," I mumbled around a mouthful of the savory sweet.

"Finest Norwegian waffles I have had," Ull agreed, spreading jam on a heart. "Now where was I?" He sat back, staring at the carved hammer above him. Seeming to reach a decision, he began.

"Kristia, I promised to tell you everything. But it is a lot to take in, and it will take time. I would like to give you an overview tonight, and if I do not scare you off, I will explain the rest this weekend. Does that sound fair?"

Anything was better than the big bag of nothing I knew right now. "Yes, it sounds fair. Now explain." Patience was never a virtue of mine.

"All right. I left town for a few days -- I needed to spend some time with my family."

"Are they okay? Is someone ill?" Of course I had the poise to be worried about his family, but I was relieved at the possibility his absence really had nothing to do with me.

"They are well, thank you. I needed to ask them a question. You see I have a certain... role that is expected of me. There is little room for flexibility in my family. I call them The Firm." He laughed bitterly and I wondered at this odd noise, such a stark contrast to the musical laughter I'd heard before. "Do not get me wrong, I love them very much and we all want what is best for one another. But there are certain realities that none of us can escape. And one of those realities is a very... dark future."

If I was right about what Ull really was, his future was as dark as it could get. "How do you mean?"

Ull thought for a moment. "How can I explain it? My family is very strong -- some of the most influential individuals in our land. But there are those who envy us and want to see us fall."

"Is this about politics?" I was determined to coax the truth out of him.

"Well, sort of. We do have substantial power. With power comes a life of duty, and in our case, a terrible demise. We cannot hold our... positions forever. And when we fall, most of us will not survive."

I struggled to keep my face neutral. My theory would account for Ull's strange behavior -- his disappearance in the club, the way he talked about his family, his stepdad's weird name. But the idea was so bizarre, I needed to hear him say it.

"Go on," I whispered.

"I do not mean to frighten you, but you have to understand what would happen if we dated. We might get sick of each other and break up next week. Or we might be perfectly suited and end up married. And if you were to become a part of my family--" he broke off. "You would suffer the same fate as the rest of us. I cannot let you die on my account." His head dropped into his hands. I could tell he wasn't upset about his own fate. He was upset that he might jeopardize mine. "So I stayed away. I did not call. It was the kindest thing to do."

I completely forgot about coaxing out a confession. My mind fixated on the *we might end up married* part. Guys our age didn't talk about marriage. Ever. And since I wasn't ready for that kind of talk, I jumped on the other end of his speech. "You seriously think leaving me hanging like that was kind?"

"Compared to getting involved with you, yes. I have a lot of what you Americans call baggage."

"Maybe." I shrugged. "But it would have been nice to know if you'd really had a good time, or if you were just saying that to get something out of me."

"Kristia." Ull smiled. "I would never knowingly hurt you. I like you far too much."

"Hold on. So you do like me?"

Ull chuckled. "Yes. I like you."

"Oh." I looked at my fingernails. "Well, sometimes I like you too. When you're not annoying me, or smothering me, or disappearing on me, or generally driving me nuts."

"That is fair." He sighed. "But it should not matter. It is not right to bring you into my life. If we end up together, you will meet the same fate that I do."

"It's not polite to speak in nonsense."

"Maybe, but there is a lot about me that you do not know."

"I'm listening." Boy howdy, was I listening.

Ull's tousled, blonde mane flopped adorably as he tilted his head. "I have not scared you off?"

I shrugged. "It takes a lot to scare me. Irritating me seems to come more naturally to you."

"Oh, Kristia." Ull lifted my hair off my neck and rested his fingers on my collarbone. I shivered. "Will you join me in the country this weekend? There is a lot I need to tell you, and it would be easier for me to get through it without interruption."

"Um... I don't think that's the best idea for us. Couldn't we just go out for dinner or something?"

"We could. But it would be best if we had more time to talk. There is much you need to know."

"Okay, two dinners then?"

"Kristia." Ull rubbed at his temples.

"Listen. You know as well as I do we haven't exactly gotten off to the greatest start. Spending a whole weekend together seems like asking for disaster, don't you think?"

"Maybe." Ull winked. "Or it might be just what we need to get on track."

Instantly, I was in an English Garden. The cobblestones at my feet formed a smallish courtyard, and candles marked a path through the ivory roses and lavender beds to a small grassy area beneath an ancient yew dale. Twinkling lights filled the dale, and Ull stood at its base with a small jewelry box in his hand, a nervous smile on his perfect face.

Mormor didn't raise no dummy. This was one vision I wanted to see for myself. Besides, I had to know if there was any truth to my ridiculous theory.

My heart pounded so fiercely that I thought it might break free from my ribcage. I pulled myself back to the present and stood without hesitation, putting my hand in Ull's.

"You win. What do I pack?"

9. ÝDALIR

"WHERE EXACTLY ARE WE going?" I asked as Ull loaded my suitcase into the back of the black Range Rover.

He winked. "A place that is very special to me. Someplace I hope you will feel right at home."

I was grateful Ull had at least told me what to pack -- comfortable clothes for weather much like this, and a pair of wellies for walks. And he'd promised to have me home in time for class on Tuesday morning -- I never signed up for Monday classes; Ardis taught me that trick freshman year.

"I am glad you came." Ull helped me into the front seat with a kiss on my cheek. My heart fluttered and I tried to remember that this was the same guy who had nearly annoyed me to death last week. I couldn't get over the shock I felt at each touch or the way my pulse spiked when I looked at him. His endless supply of fitted sweaters didn't help either. If this kept up I was going to suffer a stroke at a tragically young age.

An hour later, Ull steered the car off the main road, heading towards a collection of row houses sheathed in ivy. We followed a winding river through what I assumed was the main part of town, passing a small cobbled sign that read "Welcome to Bibury." We continued past two separate fields of sheep and drove through a small drive framed by trees until we came to a cottage.

Ull parked and got out of the car. I kept my bottom firmly planted in the passenger's seat until Ull came around and opened my door for me. I didn't want to knock him out. As a rule, I tried not to repeat my more mortifying mistakes.

He held out a hand as I stepped down, pausing next to a small fountain in the center of the drive. The cobblestone cottage had an aged roof and an unsteady-looking chimney. Soft lights from the windows welcomed us, and the smell of lavender mixed with moss filled the country air.

"It's beautiful," I breathed. It was from the pages of a fairy tale. I thought of my favorite childhood story, Cinderella, then snuck a glance at my sometimes Prince Charming. "Um, Ull? Everything all right?"

He rubbed his brow and let out a low chuckle. "I am happy you like it. I was afraid you might find it too…" he searched for the right word. "Quaint. It has been in my family for a long time." It seemed like he wanted to say more. "Come inside, Kristia. I want you to meet someone."

Ull opened the azure door and ushered me into the house. A kindly, white-haired woman in a ruffled apron flitted from the kitchen with open arms. "Ull!" A smile lit her face as she set her eyes on him. "Welcome home! Ýdalir has missed you!" Ull greeted her with a warm hug, coming back to me with a smile to match the woman's. "Ahh, I see. So this is what has kept you so busy these past few weeks. Well, let me look at you, dear."

I stepped forward shyly, feeling the woman's happy eyes on me. "Ja, ja. Vaer så god." Mormor had taught me enough Norwegian to figure out I had met the woman's approval. Ull laughed.

"Kristia, may I present Olaug. For all intents and purposes, my grandmother. She lives nearby and is good enough to take care of this cottage when I am away. We have her to thank for the lovely fire -- is that apple wood? And for what I am sure will be a delicious supper."

I held out a hand, but Olaug laughed and pulled me in for a hug. "My dear, none of that. Come you two, sit! Eat! Everything is on the table in the garden. Ull, I do hate to be rude, but I must get home to my family -- the boys are visiting for the weekend. Please come for Sunday brunch so you can meet everyone, Kristia." With a hug for each of us, she was off into the night, humming a tune that sounded vaguely familiar.

Ull smiled and closed the front door. He took my coat from my shoulders and hung it on one of the hooks below the mirror in the entry. "Well," he questioned. "Dinner or tour?"

"Tour please." I couldn't wait to see the rest of the cottage. "So what is this place?"

"This," Ull began, taking my hand and winding his fingers through mine, as comfortably as if he'd been doing it all his life, "is my country home, Ýdalir." Of course, he had a country home. And it had an even crazier name than he did. "I don't get to come here much at the moment, school being as it is this time in the term, but this is the place I feel happiest. I have much that makes me anxious, but I forget all of that when I am here." He led us down a small hallway to a study. "This is where I keep my favorite books and reading chair." He gestured to a well-worn leather loveseat and matching ottoman nestled in the corner.

"Over here," he led me to another room, containing a queen-sized four-poster bed, dresser, and writing desk, "is the guest room you will be staying in." Oh, thank God there was a guest room. I shouldn't have been surprised that Ull was the consummate gentleman, but it was still a relief to have my own room. I was already out of my element, no need to make life even scarier than it already was.

"Back here is the master suite," Ull finished simply.

Master wasn't a grand enough word. The room was huge -- considering the relatively small size of the cottage -- with an antique-looking, king-sized sleigh bed, padded bench, and built in closets that I suspected held a tiny sampling of Ull's exquisite wardrobe. Ull waited patiently as I made my way around the room, lightly touching everything to make sure it was real. I stopped when I reached the door to the bath. The jetted tub was as generously proportioned as the master suite. What the cottage offered in country charm, this bathroom offered in modern opulence.

"This is your room?"

Ull laughed. "Ah, the best is yet to come."

I seriously doubted that. But he opened the bedroom's French doors to reveal a charming garden, up-lighting illuminating the aged yew dale that had watched the house's activity for at least a hundred years. Pale roses and fragrant lavender surrounded the grassy courtyard from my earlier vision, and in the center a cobblestone patio held a table set with silver candlesticks and glowing tapers. Twinkle lights from another nearby tree added a degree of whimsy.

Ull held out a chair, and offered me the seat. He sat opposite me and opened the baking dish to reveal a hearty meal of roast, potatoes, and carrots. We ate until we were full, Ull asking about my childhood and listening with interest as I droned about the annual field trip to the lumber yard, my time spent hiking in the forests with Ardis, and how Bryan Ash beat me in the third-grade spelling bee.

He listened as if my life had been as fascinating as his must be, and I found myself revealing more and more as the evening went on. It was only when I realized that dusk was falling that I had the good sense to stop babbling. But Ull didn't seem to mind my chatter. After a generous helping of Olaug's homemade apple pie, he led me on a stroll through the garden.

We leaned with our forearms on the low, stone fence that made up the back wall, and watched the sheep grazing in the pasture behind the house. I snuck a glance at Ull and was surprised to see that he was tense. "You all right?"

He sighed. "Kristia, I have something to tell you. And I do not know if you will like it."

Well that killed the mood. "Okay." I steeled myself for the worst.

Ull took a deep breath. "Kristia, I want to share my world with you."

What did *that* mean? "Come again?"

Ull smiled. "I know, kind of out of left field, right?"

"Maybe." I tugged at the wrists of my sweater nervously. "I don't understand."

"You and I together... is a very complicated situation. And you need to know something about me before I can properly court you."

"Okay," I said as he took my hands in his. I'd never heard anyone say 'court' outside of a Jane Austen novel.

"Kristia." He drew small circles on my palms with his thumbs. I forced myself to stay standing. "Have you noticed anything different about me?"

I held my breath. If my hunch was right, Ull was about as different as anyone could possibly be. I'd been stewing on this for a week. It was the only explanation I could come up for Ull's behavior in the nightclub, the link to his stepdad, Ull's bizarre name… If it was true, and I was almost positive it was, it was so out there nobody would ever believe me. I knew I couldn't just ask Ull about it. A secret this big wasn't the kind of thing you wanted to pry out of someone. Ull had to want to tell me for himself.

"You're a pretty different guy," I evaded. "Though you do seem to have an above-average relationship with your florist."

"I am different. I am not exactly like you. I am not from here." Ull clasped his hands. He was really nervous.

"I know," I said softly.

"No, you do not. I told you I was from Norway, but that is not exactly true."

"Where are you from, Ull?" I already knew the answer. But I needed to hear it from him.

"Asgard," he whispered.

"Asgard," I repeated. I'd pretty much accepted it, but Ull's confirmation fell like a bomb. "The Asgard, Asgard."

"Yes." Ull stood still, waiting.

I exhaled. "Sif is your mom, isn't she? The Goddess of Beauty that Professor Carnicke talked about. And Thor is your stepdad."

"Yes."

"And that makes you…"

"Ull. God of Winter. Warrior and protector of Asgard." He lifted his chin an inch higher. But his eyes betrayed his fear. He had no idea how I was going to react. For the briefest of moments I contemplated the impossible.

"It's okay, Ull. I figured as much." I grabbed his hands.

"What?"

"I figured."

"How could you possibly figure a thing like that? It should seem preposterous to a human."

"I didn't say it doesn't seem preposterous. I just said I figured it out. Yesterday, when you were talking about your family and the dark future. And in the nightclub when you actually disappeared into thin air. I started to wonder about it that day in the quad when you let your dad's name slip. And you skipped town the day Professor Carnicke talked about you. Though I wasn't positive it was you at the time. Ull, you sit by me in Mythology class. *Mythology*. Not the best plan for a deity trying to fly under the radar." I shivered as I said what he was. Despite my nonchalance, I was freaking out on the inside. Ull was an actual god. What did that even mean?

"You are okay with what I am?" He held my hands tightly.

"I'm a little nervous," I admitted. "Most of my dates haven't ended with the guy telling me he's divine."

"You must have questions." Ull still looked so tense.

125

I squeezed his hands back. "Do you want to talk about it? Your Excellency?"

"Kristia--" Ull's brow furrowed and his mouth turned down.

"I'm kidding. Geez. Okay, yes, I have questions. About a million of them. Here's an easy one. Why are you here? I thought gods lived in Asgard."

"They do. We do." He took a deep breath. "It is complicated."

"I have time."

Ull nodded. "Very well. I lived in Asgard for many years. And I was destined to rule it in my grandfather's place. Doing so would have set into motion a chain of events ending in my death. I did not want to die. So I came to Midgard."

"Midgard?"

"Our name for your realm. Earth. I traveled a lot, and finally I settled in Wales." Ull touched my cheek. "It would seem I was drawn to this realm to be with you."

I blushed.

"You are not afraid of what I am?"

I should have told him I wasn't exactly normal either, with my mental tic and all. But I was too chicken. "Why are you telling me this?"

"Because I want you to know what you will be getting

into, if you choose to date me. I have been around for a very long time. But I never felt at home, until I met you. I realize that I have more baggage than almost any other man you could choose, and I promise to tell you about all of it so you can decide whether this is the life you want. Still... selfish as it is, I want to share my world with you. And I hope that, in time, you will come to feel the same way."

This could not be happening. There was no way that this god-like creature -- correction, this god -- was declaring himself to me. I couldn't begin to process what it would mean to be with him.

"This is a lot to take in."

"I know." He still gripped my hands.

"You really could have told me this over dinner in Cardiff. You didn't have to bring me all this way just to tell me you're a..." I stumbled over the word.

"A god."

"Right. That."

"And risk you running screaming from a restaurant?"

"Fair point." I held his gaze. "Well for what it's worth, I'm kind of into you too. Your Holiness."

"You have no idea how happy that makes me." His eyes crinkled and he released his hold on my hands. In one swift motion, he wrapped an arm around my lower back and lifted me off the ground so my face was even with his. His other arm hung at his side.

With cool breath, he exhaled slowly, the sweet smell making me lean in. His eyes smoldered and his lips brushed against mine as he whispered, "Thank you for not running away." He closed the small gap between us and kissed me with a force that knocked what air I had left from my chest.

I was completely unconcerned with my inability to breathe. I curled my fingers through Ull's thick hair, pulling him even closer. His arm tightened around my back, crushing my chest to his. The sensations were overwhelming.

My need for air caught up with me and I pulled back, gasping. Ull didn't release his one-armed hold so I stayed inches from his face, feet dangling off the ground. My eyes were wide as he looked at me through thick lashes.

"So how does this work, you being a god and me being, well, me?" I asked once I'd caught my breath.

Ull set me gently on my feet. My knees buckled and he helped me to the stone bench. He sat next to me, seemingly at a loss.

Ull's eyes cleared as he gave what seemed to be the best answer he could. "It means my life is a little more complicated than most. And in all likelihood my future will have a dark ending. But no matter what happens, I want to experience it with you. I have developed a deep fondness for you, Kristia Tostenson. What I am does not change that."

My cheeks were warm. "How long will you stay here? On Earth, I mean."

"As long as I can. My two closest friends are here too, Gunnar and Inga. They were unhappy with Asgard's politics when I made my decision to leave. So we came to Midgard together and have been traveling between the realms ever since, for as long as our posts will allow. We live as students so we can study at your universities. You have no idea how valuable the Environmental Studies programs have been for someone whose primary responsibility is to ensure adequate rainfall. Global warming is wreaking havoc on my job security."

"Right." I wondered if Ull knew what a poor job he was doing at blending in. "But now you're studying Classics?"

"We try to get different degrees every time we enroll," Ull explained. "Keeps things interesting." I wondered how many degrees a god could wrack up. It wasn't like they had to worry about how long it would take to graduate. Or to pay off student loans.

"How does Olaug fit into the picture? Does she know about you?"

Ull laughed, his mood lighter now that the weight of his identity was lifted. "Do you think I would be able to live as a human without someone keeping tabs on me for The Firm? Olaug is of Asgard as well. For all intents and purposes, she is my grandmother, but she also keeps me informed of the goings on back home. She lets me know when I must personally attend to my duties there. I could not have enjoyed all of these years in your realm without her."

I could have listened to Ull talk forever, but I was exhausted. I stifled a yawn as Ull gave a knowing glance. "I am sorry Kristia, I forget myself. You must sleep."

"You, uh, mustn't sleep?" I asked, echoing the formality of his words. I should have guessed that he was more than mortal. His language gave him away -- nobody in their twenties in *this* century was so proper.

"Well, yes I must sleep sometimes. I just need far less than you do to function. Immortal bodies are more efficient." He didn't say anything else on the subject, just walked me to my room and took my face in his hands. "God natt, Kristia Tostenson," he murmured. I eyed him warily, both hopeful and anxious to repeat *that kiss* -- the one that had nearly been the end of me. But he bent to kiss me chastely with the softest lips imaginable.

My disappointment must have been clear because he chuckled. "Soon enough, darling." He touched my cheek before he leaned to whisper into my ear. I caught a hint of the faintly woodsy smell that was so delicious I leaned in involuntarily. "I hope you have beautiful dreams," he murmured. With that, he walked down the hall, filling the frame of his bedroom door. With one more glance over his broad shoulder, he was gone and I was left standing with the embarrassing realization that my mouth was a little bit open. Beautiful dreams... I was pretty sure I was in one.

****

While I lay in bed that night, the rosy mist started to clear from my mind. The realities of my day settled in, much more heavily than I expected. Ull was amazing; I'd already known that. But he was also celestial -- an actual god. And while that kind of made him even more incredible, and definitely more exciting than the boys I'd known in Nehalem, it brought serious complications.

My brain, slowly lazing through its blissful fog, was beginning to grasp that this man was not meant for me. I couldn't think of any myth in which a human and a god had a successful go at a relationship. And I wasn't naïve enough to think I'd be the human to change the game.

It wasn't an ideal situation. I was falling for a man -- correction, a god -- who was totally and completely perfect, at the same time I was totally and completely human. That pairing was more than unnatural -- it was a ticking bomb. When -- and it was a matter of when, not if -- *when* Ull realized how wrong we were for each other, he would dump me faster than he could skip to the next coed or goddess or fairy princess or whoever else was lined up to date him. And then what would I do?

A worry shared is a worry halved, and there was only one person I knew with the relationship-savvy to handle this. I did the mental math. It was early evening in New York. Ardis would definitely pick up. I dialed my mobile with shaking fingers.

"Hey, girl!" Ardis answered on the first ring. "What are you doing calling me? I know, I know, you don't have FaceTime. You have got to set up your Skype. This is going to cost you a fortune!" I didn't care. Just hearing her voice made me feel better.

"Ardis," I said quietly. I didn't want Ull to hear me. "I'm so glad you answered."

"Did you get my e-mail about those shoes? Can you believe I got a pair of Louboutins at Odds & Ends?" The discount retailer had been one of our favorite haunts on our rare trips to Portland, and Ardis was still a frequent shopper of the chain in New York. "I mean, seriously -- I was so destined to have those shoes."

It was refreshing to think about something as trivial as shoes, so I asked about Ardis' shopping trip just to give my mind a break. But I knew I'd have to bite the bullet eventually, or my phone bill would be sky high.

"Ardis," I began tentatively. "I have guy problems."

"Already? You go girl! In Wales less than a month and already you're rockin' it. Wait." Her tone turned accusing. "You haven't mentioned any guys in your letters. Spill. What's his name?"

"I just started seeing this guy. His name is Ull--"

"Ull? Wow, Kristia. I have to say; you know how to pick 'em. Seriously, his name is Ull?"

"It's not exactly like I've met a whole lot of Ardises," I pointed out. "But yeah, I thought the same thing."

"Fair enough," she conceded. "So what's going on?"

"Well, we just started dating. But I'm sort of at his

country house for the weekend, and--"

Ardis' laughter rang clear across the miles. "You brazen hussy! You're spending the weekend? Who are you over there?"

"No, it's not like that. He's in his room, I'm in mine."

"Too bad." Ardis sounded disappointed. "So is that what's wrong? Not enough hanky panky?"

"Ardis!" But I hesitated. I couldn't tell Ardis the whole story. I was fairly certain Ull's... divinity -- I couldn't even think the word without twitching -- that his divinity wasn't something I should talk about. If I was vague, I could tell Ardis the most important parts and I knew she would have the words to reassure me. She always did. I dove in. "This whole relationship is happening really fast. And it's all new to me -- you know I don't have a lot of experience with this stuff."

"Tell me about it," came Ardis' dry reply.

"But I really, really like him. And he likes me back. It's crazy. He says he wants to be with me." I whispered the last part in awe.

"Then what's the problem?" Ardis was confused. So was I. Saying the words out loud made it sound so simple.

"The problem is... he's too good for me. He's smart, rich, and unbelievably gorgeous. He's got this totally adorable grandmother that he just dotes on. His family is really powerful, and way more important than me, and they live really far away and would never think in a million years

I could possibly be good enough for Ull. I mean we come from totally different worlds." That was an understatement. Asgard and Earth were as different as could be. "In the end, he's going to have to realize that there are girls out there who are better suited for him, his equal, prettier, smarter, maybe from where he's from… I don't even know where we would live if we were together, or how his family could possibly accept me, or how I could ask him to have such a boring life with me instead of the fantastic life he has by himself… but I just… really like him." My voice trailed off.

"Shhh," Ardis soothed, all bravado gone. "Kristia, sweetie, it's going to be okay. I promise. So, let me recap. You like Ull. And he likes you. And you think you want to be together. But you're afraid you're not good enough for him. Does that sum it up?"

"Yes," I said thickly into the phone.

"Sweetheart. First of all, you have got to stop thinking so little of yourself. You are an awesome woman. This Ull guy is lucky to have you, not the other way around! Don't you ever forget it." That seemed unlikely, but Ardis pushed on like the good friend she was. "Second, there isn't going to be a problem with his family. No decent parents alive would dare to disapprove of you. Not the least of which is because you are a fantastic, kind, warm-hearted girl, but also because their son has chosen you. It's parental suicide to disapprove of the girlfriend, trust me." It was true. Ardis and her womanly charms had come between more than a few sons and their mothers. "And third, none of that matters. If you guys are really that into each other, then the rest is just details. You, the biggest prude I've ever met, are spending the weekend at this guy's house. He's clearly gotten to you"

"His country house." Nobody wants to be misleading. "If we were on campus I'd go back to my flat."

"Exactly, Grandma. If you're so comfortable with him that you're already taking a trip together, he's pretty special. Everything will work out. It will. I'm not saying it will be easy, but if you guys are really that committed to each other, it would take a lot more than the stuff you're afraid of to keep you apart. So relax."

My world had righted itself once again. Ardis always knew what to say. "Thank you Ardis. You're the best friend I've ever had." My eyes felt dewy. "I miss you."

"Aw, I miss you too, girl! I can't wait to see you after you graduate." Since I'd taken extra courses each semester, plus done summer sessions, I would finish ahead of Ardis. She was coming to visit in May so we could spend part of our summer together. "I've never been to Europe!"

"Well we *are* from Nehalem. We're not exactly world travelers."

"Not yet!" Ever the optimist. "Oops. I have to go -- my date's here. But e-mail me when you get back to school and tell me how the weekend went. Try to have some *fun*." She emphasized the last word and I could imagine her wiggling her eyebrows suggestively. The knot in my chest felt considerably looser as we got off the phone. Ardis' words always hit home. I liked Ull -- a lot. And he liked me. The rest was just stuff to be handled together. But exactly how much 'stuff' came along with dating a Norse god?

10. ULL MYHR

BY MORNING, MY OVERWORKED brain was moving like a herd of turtles. Ardis had helped me through my hysteria, but I was still coming up with every possible reason this relationship was doomed. I was too beat to indulge in a freak-out. Mormor always said there was no point in borrowing trouble. Besides, Ull kept me too busy to worry by showing me around Bibury.

"I think I need new rainboots." I padded into the library in a fresh pair of socks. My first pair got soaked in the downpour that ended our walk.

"You think?" Ull held up a blanket and patted the couch next to him. I settled into the spot.

"Nice fire." I was impressed. He'd set it up *and* made two cups of tea in the time it had taken me to change.

"I am God of Winter. I should be good for something."

"Glad to know you're not slacking just because you're on vacation."

"Oh Kristia, I am never on vacation. Odin can summon me at any time." He pulled my legs across his lap. "Though I do consider it my duty to protect you from the elements raging outside."

"Well protect away, Your Holiness." My wisecrack was drowned by a clap of thunder. "Is that your family calling?"

"Funny, Kristia."

"I thought so." Laughing was easier than thinking about how absurd our situation actually was. The cutest guy on campus moonlighted as a fierce Asgardian warrior. Not exactly the hobby I'd imagined my first serious boyfriend would have.

"Can I ask you more questions?" I rested my head on his shoulder and watched the rain pelt the window.

"Ask away."

"How did you end up God of Winter?" It seemed like a softball question. But when Ull froze, I realized I'd touched on a nerve. I made myself very interested in my fingernails. "Sorry, that was personal. It's none of my business."

"No, I want to tell you. I just want you to know the man I am now, not the killer I used to be." It was my turn to freeze, but I pushed the feeling down, desperate to know everything.

"I don't understand."

Ull's shoulders dropped. "I am not a particularly upstanding man, Kristia."

"I don't believe that."

"You should. I have done heinous things -- things you could not imagine. I have killed thousands -- not that they did not deserve it. I tortured uncooperative hostiles in the name of interrogation. And pursuing you like this when I know what my fate holds... I have no right to be with you."

"Ull, believe me. I'm not perfect either." In fact, I was all kinds of crazy, but this didn't seem like the time to dive into my mental problem.

"You are kind to me." Ull lifted a finger to my cheek.

"So how did you come to be this terrible guy?" I raised a teasing eyebrow. "You seem more the puppy-dog type at the moment." Ull blinked.

"I was born to be a warrior. My mother is the most accomplished warrior goddess of all time. Not only does she hold the most kills of any female, but her accuracy is unmatched." Well butter my flapjacks, my boyfriend's mom was a trained killer. "My father died in battle before I reached school age. When my mother remarried, we moved in with Thor."

"Scary stepdad?" I turned my palms to lace my fingers through Ull's.

"At times. But he was also a tremendous resource. Before I became God of Winter, I was part of the Elite Team -- Asgard's top assassins."

"How was that?"

"It was... tolerable... until a target begged for his life. Said he had children waiting at home. That was the turning point. I set the target free and asked Odin for a new post."

"What did he say?"

"He was displeased. But I became God of Winter and have served there since. I took a short break once." His face darkened. "But I came back."

"And now you're here."

Ull winked at me, and my insides felt very sloshy. "I like living in your realm."

"Why?" I'd take Asgard over Nehalem in a heartbeat.

"Because I can be myself here. My pull to this realm has always been a mystery. Perhaps all along I was waiting for you to show up." He touched my chin and brought my lips to his. I lifted my hand to his cheek. His stubble prickled my palm. I let my other hand rest on his arm, and trailed my fingers along his bicep. He pressed against me, deepening the kiss. My head spun and my face burned in the firelight. I pressed back, and climbed into his lap. Ull gently pushed me away and I opened my eyes.

"You don't have to stop." My breath was uneven.

"I do. You do not know enough about me to decide whether you want to be with me."

"I want to be with you. Honest." It wasn't just the

hormones talking. I really liked him.

"You say that now." He chuckled. "Shall we continue our discussion? I am sure you have more questions."

"Okay, fine." I waited for the blood to move back up to my brain. Apparently I didn't wait long enough, because I heard myself blurt out, "Why were you so mean to me in the British Museum?"

"I do not know what you are talking about."

"Come on, Ull. Give me more credit than that." I stared at him until he blinked.

"Because I knew who you were."

"You knew I was Kristia Tostenson?"

"No. I knew you were meant to be my wife." I pulled back, but Ull quickly wrapped both arms around me. "No, please. Just listen."

I slowly resumed blinking.

"Remember the first day of class, when Professor Carnicke talked about the Norns?"

"The prophets," I whispered.

"Correct. Well, you and I shared the same Norn. Her name was Elsker -- the name means Love in Norwegian. She prophesied I would be a Warrior, live alone and give my life for my people. When you were born, my future changed. Elsker said if I wanted to take a partner I could find you at Cardiff in twenty years."

"And... marry me."

"Eventually, yes."

"That doesn't explain why you were so mean to me. If anything, I'd think you'd be nice to the person who was supposed to spare you from what sounds like a really depressing life."

"I was not finished."

"Oh. Sorry, Your Excellency."

"Kristia," Ull growled.

"Okay, okay. Finish."

"I was mean to you because, despite Elsker's prophecy, there is an absolute ban on Asgardian-Mortal relationships. The Norns are forbidden from mingling the fates of gods and mortals. Elsker broke the rule. I would never have turned her in, but we have this... questionable figure in Asgard. Loki. He found out what Elsker did and she was banished for her betrayal. I never got to talk to her again."

"That's terrible."

"I was mean to you because I knew that even though we were meant to be together, we never could be. Odin would never allow our relationship. Besides, I am fated to die with the rest of my family, so it is not like we could have any sort of a happy ever after. It hurt to be so close to you and to know I could not have you."

"Oh, Ull." I rested my head on his shoulder. "I had no

idea."

"How could you? I did not explain."

"I know, but... I'm still sorry."

"No, I am sorry. I hurt you. But honestly, it was never my intention to do anything but protect you."

"I see that now." I squeezed his arm. "Can I ask another question?"

"Shoot."

"What really happened during the time you were away?" He'd obviously kept a lot from me.

Ull laughed sharply at being called out. "I was telling the truth when I told you I had gone to see my family, to see whether I could be with you without endangering your life. Getting a straight answer from them was complicated."

"How do you mean?"

"Listen Kristia, I do not feel right asking you to join me in a life that I do not completely want to be a part of myself. My death is inevitable. Our enemies want to kill every Asgardian -- we have certainly killed enough of their kind. It is terrible to know that you will lose the people you love -- and that you will die yourself. Losing my father was hard enough, the thought of losing my friends and my mother is incomprehensible. And to lose you -- it would be more than I could handle." Ull's eyes filled with pain and it struck me how sensitive he actually was.

I'd been so wrong about him. He didn't keep everyone at arm's length because he was uppity -- he did it so he wouldn't get hurt. What an isolating existence. "It has been one thing to know my death is marked, but to ask you to voluntarily give your life -- I am not worth that price."

I was starting to think there were a dozen reasons he was wrong, but I bit my tongue.

"Unfortunately for you, I can be selfish. I wanted to be with you. But like I said, no god has ever been allowed to marry a mortal. Thor certainly was not going to sign off on it -- he fancies another warrior for my wife, and he would never understand that I allowed myself to fall in love."

"Super." This wasn't sounding so good.

"But my mother understands how I feel about you, and she sent me to my friend Inga's father. Jens is Odin's chief advisor, and my mother thought he might be able to help us."

"I'm liking your mom." Ull smiled and my stomach fluttered.

"I ran into Balder on my way. He serves as our judge. I asked him whether it would be wrong to invite you to join me in this existence."

"Ull," I interrupted, but he shook his head.

"I have much guilt in that Kristia. If Balder had said it was wrong, then I would have left you alone, difficult as it would have been. But Balder was generous."

"Okay, now I'm liking this Balder guy too." Not only because I felt bad for the poor fellow whose parents had burdened him with the name of Balder.

"By the time I saw Jens, my mind was mostly made up. I would court you and see whether you would share my life with me. But no human had ever been to Asgard, and to my knowledge, no god had ever taken up permanent residence on Earth. I needed Jens to help me with some of the... eh, technical issues."

Suddenly, I was in an unfamiliar world. I instinctively knew it was Asgard in the distant past. Two robed men walked angrily down a long hallway. Columns supported the roof, the open-aired walls overlooking a pristine village.

"It is an abomination," the taller of the men snapped. He wore an eye patch and his long white hair streamed behind his hurried pace.

"Odin," the other man placated. He was rushing to keep up. "This was bound to happen sooner or later. They are not that different from us."

"They are nothing like us!" Odin thundered in fury. "Asking me to admit a human to Asgard?" He practically spit the words. "It is unheard of, Jens. No human is fit to enter here. The Fates are fools to cast our lot for the betterment of Midgard."

Jens' robe quivered. He darted his eyes around the hallway as if someone might be watching. "Odin, you must not speak ill of the Fates. And you should not speak ill of Earth. You know the prophecy."

"Yes. Asgard shall fall to save Midgard -- Earth, as you so

lovingly call it. Perhaps you want to move there like your daughter?"

Jens fell silent.

Odin inhaled. His shoulders rose with effort. "I am sorry. I should not speak against Inga. And I should not speak against the Fates. But I will never, as long as I exist, agree Asgardian lives should be lost so Midgard can prosper. When Ragnarok comes it will be a travesty -- the loss of a superior race of beings for the survival of mortals should never have been prophesied so lightly."

Oh, super. Now my visions were checking into the past too. Was there no end to the depths of my lunacy?

Ull's voice pulled me back. He didn't seem to realize I'd been somewhere else. "I would rather not go into detail, but suffice to say Odin is not mankind's biggest fan."

"I see."

"I cannot bring you back to Asgard as my mate, but that does not preclude our being together. I can stay here as yours. Another warrior fell in love with a human a long time ago. He chose to live as a mortal rather than be without her." So that's what Odin was so angry about in my apparition.

"Oh, crimeney. But you're not saying that you would--" Ull interrupted with a finger to my lips.

"Now before you get upset, hear me out. It makes sense for me to join your world. I like living here. You will not have to give up anything to be with me. We can live a long and happy human life together, ideally passing on before Asgard's enemies ever attack. There is no downside."

"No downside?" If he'd put it any differently, I could have kept my temper.

"I had just returned from Asgard the night you were attacked. You needed me, for your own protection, if not my selfish desire. And I need you. So here we are." Ull seemed unaccountably pleased with himself.

My fuming wasn't silent for long.

"So here we are? Are you insane?" How could he think this was a good idea? "You want to give up your immortality to be with me? Absolutely not. Forget it." There was more wrong with this than a bull in a henhouse.

"Shh," Ull soothed. If he'd thought his decision would make me happy, he obviously didn't know the first thing about me. "Darling, this is not your choice to make."

"Everything is not all about you, you know. This affects me too!"

"I know it does. And for the record, my life has never been about me."

"What's that supposed to mean? Are you trying to make me feel sorry for you? Because it's not going to work."

"Not much works on you, does it?"

"Nope."

"Well, I am not trying to make you feel anything. Being

147

of Asgard requires a life of duty and service -- it is just the way things are."

"So?" The sympathy card wasn't going to get him far.

"So, every choice I have ever made, everything I have ever done, right down to who I associate with, has been affected by what I am. Being with you... this is the first decision of my existence based solely on what I want. I am not giving up anything I do not want to. I need to be with you. Whether I am a god or a human is inconsequential so long as you are by my side. The rest will work itself out in time."

"I'm not going to be the reason you have to give up who you were born to be!" Leave it to me to bring down an actual god. This was all kinds of wrong.

"Darling, please do not be upset. Everything will be all right. I have been alone as a god for a very long time. I would much rather be a human with you than ghost along without you." He held me while I buried my head in his shoulder, outraged by the unfairness of our situation. Ull might have thought he had made his decision, but I would find another way out of this. He was not going to abandon the most basic part of him. I wouldn't let him.

****

At the end of the night, I was exactly where I wanted to be -- standing outside the guest room with my fingers wrapped in Ull's hair and my lips pressed against his. I was dizzy and I knew I would have fallen over if Ull wasn't holding me so close.

So it was more than just disappointing when he pulled back. It was dangerous.

"You don't have to stop." I grabbed onto his sweater to interrupt my fall.

"I do, actually." He guided me back to standing. "My mother raised me well."

"Meaning…"

"Meaning you are not my wife yet. So I do have to stop."

"Seriously?" I didn't see that one coming.

"Mortals." Ull chuckled. "So impatient." He kissed me softly on the cheek. "God natt, Miss Tostenson. I shall see you in the morning." It took everything I had not to stomp my foot. He walked down the hall and closed his bedroom door behind him.

That god was going to drive me crazy.

****

My Ragnarok nightmare returned that night, so vivid I couldn't be sure this one wasn't actually a vision.

I saw the battlefield as a spectator; mercifully, no giant wolf or snake could reach me from whatever vantage point I'd claimed. The field was carpeted with lavender, the air filled with its subtle scent. Ull stood dead center, facing the inevitable attack. In the distance, the tree-trunk snake and the oversized predator stalked towards their prey. Their slanted eyes were filled with hatred.

I wanted to scream at Ull to save himself, but he was as hungry for this fight as the creatures were hungry for Asgardian blood. There wasn't a trace of emotion as he dropped to a hunting crouch, tensed for the battle he was fated to lose. The monsters were fifty yards away now, picking up speed as they locked Ull in their sights. The wolf bowed his head and charged, trampling the flowers beneath his feet as he thundered towards the man who owned my heart. With twenty yards between them, Ull poised to spring at Death, determination across his angry brow. So this was it -- I had to watch while my beloved ran headfirst to meet his end.

Then I saw the scene from a fresh perspective. A strong, confident woman stood with Ull, poised to launch her own attack. I knew instinctively she could protect him. Her fists were clenched as she crouched to strike and she wore the long, white robes of an Asgardian warrior. She was no more concerned for her fate than Ull was for his, and she sprinted furiously towards the attackers, leaping at the open jaws to wrestle the wolf to the ground.

As I focused in on her face, I sat up with alarm, grasping at my bed sheets in the darkness. She was me.

11. BACK TO SCHOOL

AFTER THE WEEKEND WE'D had, going back to Cardiff was almost surreal. Of course I was sworn to secrecy about Ull's heritage, so quick thought was required when Victoria and Emma pounced.

"Kristia," Emma teased as I walked in on Monday evening. "You left with Ull, *days* ago." She overemphasized the word. "What on earth have you been doing all this time?"

Victoria jumped up on the couch, tucking her long legs beneath her. "Yes, do tell. What, where, how many times…" My face must have complimented the burgundy door pretty well.

"No, no. Nothing like that! Nothing inappropriate went on. Ull is old-fashioned." Very old-fashioned. Nobody did old-fashioned like the Vikings.

"Right." Victoria raised one perfectly-groomed eyebrow at Emma.

Emma winked back. "I'm sure you had a glorious time studying together and discussing the British Economy. Where exactly did you say he took you?"

"To his family home in the Cotswolds." I jumped at the opportunity and dove into a detailed description of the garden at Ýdalir, Bibury's duck pond, and Olaug's amazing food. "But the house was the most impressive thing."

"More impressive than Ull's arms?" Emma teased.

"OK, the second most impressive thing."

"More than Ull's chest?" Victoria was quick to reply.

"OK, the house was the most impressive thing, not counting Ull himself." This stumped them momentarily, and I rushed along. "It's an amazing cottage that belongs in a fairytale. It has this long driveway, a little fountain in the middle and the sweetest little chimney that puffs smoke like a cartoon. The garden backs up to this pasture with actual sheep, and the sitting room has big couches to watch the rain. It's like a piece of heaven." Or a piece of Asgard, though from what Ull had told me they were pretty much the same.

"It does sound… impressive," Emma begrudgingly admitted. "But you really don't have anything juicier to share? Come on, K! Spill, are you two, like, dating?"

Dating. It seemed so ordinary a word -- it didn't exactly cover Ull's pledge to share his world with me, or my secret plot to circumvent Asgard's ban on humans. But dating would have to do.

"Yes. We're dating." I flushed.

"You go, girl. A month into the semester and you've snagged the most eligible bachelor on campus." Victoria sighed with satisfaction. "I told you your outfit was perfect."

Emma laughed. "Leave it to Victoria to make it all about clothes!"

****

Once my roommates were asleep, I closed my door and booted up my laptop. I'd left Ýdalir with more questions than answers, thanks to the discovery that my boyfriend was a god -- an Asgardian assassin no less. I knew he'd given me all the information he was willing to share for now, so I felt only a little guilty turning to the Internet for answers.

Google did not disappoint. I typed in "Norse gods" and came up with a slew of websites relaying the stories Mormor had told me as a child. There was Sif, the Warrior Goddess of Beauty. And Thor, all-powerful with his mighty Mjölnir. Odin was there in his eye patch and even Balder was represented, bearing a masculine resemblance to our own Lady Justice. Each god had a story to tell, and for an hour, I lost myself in their journeys. How different this studying was, knowing these myths were about real people.

Next, I entered "Ull Myhr" and came up with nothing,

so I dropped the Myhr and got a whole range of pages. I found everything from some ski festival in Breckenridge honoring the snow god, to a runic drawing of a man on old-fashioned skis -- or were they skates? -- crossing a river. There were academic papers detailing Ull's parentage, and even a blurb about his rumored assassination by Danes after taking over for Odin. According to the Internet everything Ull had told me about himself was true. But I'd known that much. What I didn't know was how he fared at Ragnarok.

I switched gears, searching for Ragnarok. Everything I found was pretty consistent with what Mormor and Professor Carnicke had preached. The realms would turn on Asgard, with serpents and wolves and every imaginable beast attacking the gods and destroying the earth. Nearly all the gods would die horrible deaths, with an unnamed handful either surviving or being reborn.

Well that was no help. I wanted names. I wanted to see that Ull was going to live. I clicked the next link, then the next, but nothing could tell me who might survive. Ull wasn't even mentioned in the Ragnarok articles. For the first time in my life, the Internet had failed to provide me with the information I needed.

I closed the computer and lay my cheek against its casing. None of this made any sense. According to the Internet, my highly accredited University course, and every story I'd ever been told, Ragnarok had already happened. The Earth was reborn from the aftermath, and descendents of the survivors repopulated the planet. So why was Ull talking like Ragnarok was some looming threat, a to-be-determined gala of destruction? Wasn't it in the past? Obviously I didn't know everything about the End of the World. And neither did the Internet. Problem was, I didn't have anyone else to ask. Ull was the only god I knew, and I wasn't about to question him on what I knew was a very sensitive issue. I crawled into bed and hoped some rest would slow the fears gnawing at my brain.

****

My night was quiet, but my sleep was fitful. Usually, my dreams were filled with visions of Ragnarok or creepy Elf Man or other scary things, but tonight I was replaying my last night at Ýdalir. Ull walked me to my door and declined my romantic overture, just like he had in real life. But in my dream, I tilted my head and stuck out my lower lip.

"Ull," my pout was seriously unladylike, "It's just one more kiss. What's the big deal?"

"Kristia, I cannot," Ull demurred. "You have to understand."

"Oh, I understand all right." I took a step closer, inhaling his woodsy scent. "I understand that you kissed me so thoroughly you're afraid if you do it again, you'll lose control and do something crazy. Is that right?" I trailed a finger through his thick hair, down his jaw, and along the line of his torso and rested my palm flat against his abs.

"That is right," Ull breathed softly. His eyes burned

with longing.

"Good," I whispered into his ear. "I want you to do something crazy." I took a step closer and he wrapped an arm around my waist. "Please, Ull. Just another minute. Then I swear, I'll leave you alone."

He lowered his face to mine, kissing me with such determination I lost all sense of time and space. "Do not ever leave me alone," he growled and backed me into the guest room.

Against my will, I was sucked out of my dream, back to the tiny room where I lay tangled in my sheets. I was positive my face was so bright I could have made a living as a landing beacon. And I was equally certain my grandmother would have died all over again if she'd had any idea what I was capable of.

****

When Ull showed up to walk me to class the next morning, I had a hard time looking him in the eye. I wasn't sure what had come over me the night before, though I had to admit my feminine wiles had impressed me. I wondered when I'd work up the nerve to do something like that in real life.

Today wouldn't be the day. My consummate gentleman came to my door holding a single ivory rose.

"Good morning, Kristia." he handed me the stem.

"Morning." I blushed. "This is beautiful. Thanks." I ducked inside to put it in water. It brought some cheer to our tiny kitchen.

"Anything for you." He took my umbrella as I closed the door behind me. We started walking towards campus. "Speaking of which, I went ahead and ordered you a pair of Hunters. Size six, right?"

"My feet? Yes, six. What are Hunters?"

"Wellies," he clarified. I stared blankly. "Rainboots."

"Oh. Oh! Wow, thank you. That was really nice."

"It was time."

"Ha ha." I glanced at my feet. He wasn't wrong. This pair had seen better days.

"Did you get any of the Mythology reading done last night?"

I blushed. I'd read about mythology all right, but not the text Professor Carnicke had assigned. "Um, no. I was sort of hoping having a Norse god for a tutor would give me an edge."

"So you expect me to be your tutor now?"

"Among other things."

"Oh, Miss Tostenson. What am I going to do with you?" Ull took my hand and we walked to class.

"Sit with me, for starters." I slid into the third row and waved at my usual seatmate. "Henry, this is Ull Myhr. Ull, this is my friend Henry Webster."

"Cheers, Ull. Nice to meet you." Henry stuck out his hand.

"Henry." Ull's nod was curt.

"Relax," I whispered as I got out my laptop. "We're just friends."

"I know," Ull spoke a little too quickly.

"Seriously Ull, you're threatened by *him*?"

"I am nothing of the sort." Ull got out his notebook and clicked the top of his pen. He threw an arm around me with feigned nonchalance, clenching his jaw at Henry's oblivious smile.

How cute.

After class we headed to the Student Union for tea. Ull's mobile rang insistently as I poured milk in my drink. "Sorry darling," he murmured, brushing my forehead with his lips. "It is Olaug. I must take this. Meet you outside." He grabbed his cup and strode to the door, speaking in Norwegian. It was really hot when he did that -- even though I could never keep up with the words.

I took my time adding the sugar and headed outside. When I got to Ull, he'd closed his mobile and was staring at the clouds.

"How is everything?"

"Hmm?" He turned to me. "Oh. Fine." In girl-speak, "fine" never means "fine." But I wasn't fluent in Norse-god.

"'Fine' -- Sunday supper might be chicken instead of roast, 'fine', or 'fine' -- Ýdalir is infested with rodents and I need an Asgardian assassin here pronto to wipe them out, 'fine'?"

"Do not worry yourself, darling," Ull kissed the top of my head casually as we walked to the library. "Olaug was only giving me a status report. The Norns do not see any threats to Asgard until summer, though they are vague on *which* summer will spark the trouble."

I had pretty much accepted that a lot of Ull's behavior was cryptic, that many things he did would be mysterious at best, unnerving at worst. I tried to be okay with this. Dating a god wasn't easy, but the way I felt about Ull was worth the uncertainty about our future. He handed me my tea and we walked to the library, deep in our own thoughts. Ull broke the silence once we'd settled into the coveted leather chairs next to the fireplace.

"Would you like to double-date with my roommates this weekend?"

"Gunnar and Inga? Um, sure. That sounds nice." I knew it was a ploy to distract me, but it worked. I was pretty easily distracted these days. Gunnar and Inga were gods -- what would we talk about? Would they be as easy to be around as Ull? Why were they here? Was it just to support their friend? That obsessive part of my brain normally devoted to school took over, and I forgot all about Ull's conversation with Olaug. He smiled as he leaned back in his chair, immersing himself in his textbook while my mind went into overdrive.

12. GUNNAR AND INGA

I'VE NEVER HAD A harder time dressing than I did the night of our double date with Gunnar and Inga. Victoria was ready to kill me by the time she finally shooed me out the door.

"No, Kristia, Listen to me! You cannot wear that blouse. It says 'I am trying too hard. I want you to like me.' You must wear this dress. It says, 'I am easygoing and fun. No high maintenance here. Oh, but oops -- I'm also really cute and quite clever.'"

"The dress says all that?" Emma was dumbfounded.

"It does." Victoria nodded sagely.

"Fine." I snatched the dress from her hands and pulled off my blouse, not caring what I wore anymore. I'd tried on at least fifteen different outfits and none of them felt good enough to wear to meet Ull's friends. This was another situation on which the etiquette police were silent.

"Do you have your conversation points ready?" With the aid of the Internet, Emma had helped me brainstorm a list of appropriate topics to discuss when meeting one's boyfriend's friends. She'd even diagrammed them onto a spreadsheet. I'd been studying it all day.

"Yes." I ticked them off from memory. "What are your classes? How did you choose Cardiff? Where are you from?" Okay, obviously that one wasn't going to make the cut. *How is the weather in Asgard this time of year, if I may ask?* "What sports do you like? Have you ever been to Oregon? Seriously Emma, I don't know about that last one. I'm pretty sure they've never been anywhere near Nehalem."

"True." She nodded. "But it will give them the chance to ask you about your home, and if you haven't been contributing to the conversation, then you'll be able to sparkle." She winked. "You're going to do fine, Kristia."

Fine as a fish in a bear's claw. The thought of meeting Ull's friends had me wound so tight, I jumped at the knock on the door.

"Yes, fine. Bye!" Victoria all but pushed me out the door and into the surprised arms of my date. I smiled nervously.

As Ull drove me to the pub where we were meeting his friends, he explained that Gunnar and Inga were his only confidantes here. His circle of human companions was limited to me.

"Despite my choice to live in your realm, I keep your kind at arm's length -- I generally try to follow Asgardian law. Gunnar and Inga were the only ones I was able to confide in here, until I met you."

My nerves melted a little bit -- I was secretly pleased to be the first mortal he'd ever welcomed into his life. Ull was very guarded, and it was a big deal to be let in.

"So if our futures can't mix, then by dating you, am I making you a criminal?"

"Pretty much." He grinned.

"What do your friends think about that?" I grinned back. Kristia Tostenson, outlaw. Ardis would have been so proud. Mormor might have felt a little differently.

"They are oddly supportive."

"Tell me about them." In a matter of minutes, I'd be face to face with two more Norse gods. As my nerves had removed all memory of Emma's carefully crafted conversation points, I needed something to talk with them about besides the weather. Or heaven forbid, the cleanliness of Cardiff. I was *not* going down that road again.

"Well, Gunnar is my oldest friend. He has come with me to most of the universities I have attended in Europe, and a few in the States. He is a tremendous athlete and an even better fighter." By now, we'd reached the restaurant. "And here he is. Gunnar!" I recognized him from my first night at Cardiff. Gunnar was tall and muscular like Ull, with chocolate-brown hair that stood in spikes around a tanned face. He had twinkling, green eyes that made him seem mischievous. I liked him immediately.

He stood when we reached the table and met Ull with a hearty clap on the back.

"So this is the lass who's tamed our bachelor!" Gunnar reached out to grab me in a warm hug. "It's nice to finally meet you!"

"Here, here." Inga rose and reached across the table to shake my hand in welcome. She was willowy and slim, with long white-blonde hair that swayed as she moved. Her cheekbones were prominent and her enormous blue eyes managed to sparkle, even in the dim lighting. She was the prettiest girl I'd ever seen in real life -- maybe even as beautiful as those girls in the fancy bra advertisements. "It's nice to meet you Kristia." She sat back down with inhuman grace. It was like watching water dance.

"Nice to meet you too." If that was what a goddess looked like, why on Earth was Ull dating me? It was hard not to feel inferior.

"It's so nice to finally get to go on a double date. Ull here has made himself quite the third wheel for way too long."

Ull glared at Inga, who shot him an angelic face.

At her words, I was in a tastefully-decorated living room. The silver-framed photos on the mantel held pictures of Inga, Gunnar, and Ull in various states of amusement -- laughing on top of a ski slope, straddling mountain bikes in a forest. Inga was coming out of a doorway I could only assume was a kitchen, carrying a square plate of delicious smelling pastries. She offered me one before curling up on the couch, tucking her long legs beneath her as she sat.

My insecurities faded a little as I pulled myself out of my vision. Despite her celestial beauty, Inga and I were going to be good friends.

"Oh, Inga. You have always been so patient to put up with me." Ull rolled his eyes good-naturedly as he picked up his menu.

"I have, haven't I?" Inga winked at me. The discussion moved on to what to eat, then fell easily into the banter of old friends. When Gunnar and Inga rose to visit their respective powder rooms, I turned to Ull.

"Sorry, I know this is tacky, but I have to ask. If that's what goddesses look like what are you doing dating a human?"

"Kristia." His cool breath blew on my ear. "You are the loveliest creature I have laid eyes on. From the moment I saw you, nothing could have kept me from your side." His finger slid from my ear down my neck, tickling it with a feather-light touch that made my eyes roll closed. He grazed my jaw with his teeth, sending shivers up and down my back. "I have never been in love before, and to think I nearly missed out on this because I was stubborn."

My eyes flew open.

"Yes, darling. I am in love with you. Completely, madly, head over heels in love with you. Surely you knew?"

I blushed. "I think I did. But it's nice to hear the words anyway." I looked at my hands, then forced myself to meet Ull's eyes. "I'm in love with you too, you know," I confessed.

"I know." Ull pressed his lips against mine and I breathed in his pine scent. I could have stayed there forever.

Gunnar's deliberate cough brought me back to reality. He and Inga slid into the booth. "Sorry to interrupt, but the food's here." Gunnar graciously steered the conversation towards our classes, asking Inga about a term paper she was working on.

"It's nearly finished," her melodic voice paused, "I just need to talk to my professor about a formatting question."

"Is it Professor Krups?" Gunnar grimaced.

"That's right, you had him last term." Inga tilted her head, her blonde hair shaking softly around her shoulders. "How could I forget?"

"Great Odin, Inga. How could you forget?" Ull rolled his eyes.

"Just about drove me mad," Gunnar muttered. Turning to me he explained, "He marked me down half a grade on my final paper for using the wrong font. The wrong font. Who bloody cares about a font?"

"Professor Krups." Inga nodded knowingly. "I had the same thing happen on my first paper, so I want to make sure I've got all my I's dotted and my T's crossed."

"I'm sorry, who is this professor?"

Ull turned to me. "I have not had the privilege of

studying under Professor Krups. But I have heard an earful from these two over the past year, and apparently he is a stickler for the little things."

"Just jealous because he couldn't have come up with anything so original," Gunnar grumbled to Inga's amusement.

"Still sore, darling?"

"A font," was all he replied. It was reassuring to hear gods complain about grades and teachers. Maybe this was going to be easier than I'd thought.

Though I wanted desperately to ask Ull's friends about their life outside Cardiff, talk moved to plans for the winter holiday. We only got two weeks of vacation and Gunnar and Inga were going skiing. I'd planned to stay in Cardiff to get a head start on my reading, but Ull proposed a different idea as we were driving home.

"I was wondering if you might join me at Ýdalir for Christmas. I was planning to leave after St. Lucia's Day -- are you familiar with the holiday?"

"Of course." Mormor had celebrated it every year. "The Scandinavian celebration of light."

"And strength." Ull paused, no doubt thinking of the young saint. Her spirit had been so strong she overcame death.

"And strength," I agreed.

"Well, the mass at our church is beautiful. Inga is going

167

to be this year's Lucia of course. We could head to Bibury after the service, spend the holiday in the country. What do you say?"

"Um, yes. Absolutely, yes." Two weeks alone with Ull sounded very nice. Maybe I could even channel my bolder dream-self to make a move on him. I giggled. My life was so different than it had been a few months ago.

"What is it, my love?" Ull asked of my laugh.

"I'm just happy. For someone who spent pretty much her whole life looking for a place to belong, this is pretty great. I mean... I didn't have any siblings, I was always too shy to make a lot of friends, and as much as I like Nehalem, I didn't exactly fit in." Nothing prohibits assimilation like the whole hamlet thinking you're a loon. "I spent twenty years feeling like I was watching my life play out without ever really living it. But then I met you, and everything just clicked into place. It's like I'm finally home." I clapped my hand over my mouth, embarrassed by my honesty. When we slowed for a stoplight Ull pulled it away.

"Kristia, darling, in all my years, this is the first time I have felt I was where I was meant to be. I am so very *lucky* that I met you." Blushing fiercely, I was the first to break eye contact and we drove in silence, our intertwined fingers linking us together.

****

"Hello Poppett." Oh, jumping Jezebel. I'd know that voice anywhere, though I'd only heard it twice.

"Goodbye, Elf Man." I didn't bother opening my eyes. My previous dream had been very enjoyable, and I wasn't terribly pleased this new one interrupted it. "Kindly see yourself out of my head please." No point in being rude, even to an imaginary creature.

"As you wish." The hissing voice was followed by a snap. I settled comfortably into my blankets, glad I hadn't wasted any energy opening my eyes. The cold wind on my face gave me pause. Unless my window was open... oh, crimeney. The dream wasn't over. I wasn't in my bedroom anymore. Based on the big tree to my right, I was pretty sure my bed was now in the garden at Ýdalir. I sat up.

"Fine, I'll play. But make it snappy Elfie, I'm really tired." My brain was obviously more messed up than I thought.

"Oh, I can be very fast." The keening sound was to my right and when I turned he was against me, wrapping a rope around my neck and pulling it taut. The rough fibers cut into my throat. I tried to breathe in, but the movement was painful and pointless.

"I warned you I would come for you if you tried to join him." The pointy-eared man sneered. "I can't have you spoiling my plan." A kick to my stomach evicted what little breath I had left, and my lungs collapsed. I clawed at the rope but the crazed man was too strong. His cackling echoed through the fog that crept across my brain. I was slipping under -- it would be death by strangulation this time.

I swatted feebly at the rope and as I did my finger caught on Mormor's necklace. I made a weak fist around it, something comforting to hold in my final moment. Suddenly, my hand was hot and a bright light forced my eyelids closed. I sensed, rather than saw, that the radiance came from my hand -- the silver hammer was exploding with luminosity. Beams shot directly into my attacker.

He pulled back to save himself, dropping the rope as he did so. I gulped in cold air, filling my lungs over and over. I could hear his sickening screech as he stumbled backwards, the light piercing his chest with a flood of arrows. He grabbed at the beams to pull them out, but I sensed he was losing the battle. I couldn't know for sure, because in the next moment I was back in my room, covered in sweat and clinging to the necklace that had saved my life. When I opened my hand the hammer was glowing.

****

I didn't see the Elf Man again while I was at Cardiff. I did, however, decide I needed to see Ull again. Right away. Something really strange was happening, and I didn't want to deal with the visions on my own anymore. Ull had been forthcoming with me and I had no reason not to trust him with my secret.

"Kristia. Are you all right?" I thought I'd waited until a

decent hour to call, but I guess normal college students aren't up at 7:00 a.m. on the weekend.

"Um, yes. No. I don't know. Can you come over?"

"Of course. I will be right there."

"You don't have to rush or anything…" I trailed off. Please, please rush. I needed to get this off my chest.

"I am on my way."

Twenty minutes later, Ull knocked. "I would have been here sooner, but I figured you could use breakfast."

"Earl grey." I took the cup gratefully.

"And chocolate croissants." Ull carried the bag to the coffee table and sat in the corner of the couch. I grabbed a thick blanket and curled up next to him.

"You are up early for a Sunday." Ull wasn't very good at hiding his anxiety. Well that was okay -- neither was I.

"Do you remember when you told me about our Norn, Elsker?" I clutched my tea. I'd never actually come out and admitted what I could do to anyone. Mormor had just always known, and she'd told Ardis for me when we were little. The rest of Nehalem could only guess at the weirdness in my head -- I certainly wasn't spelling it out for them.

"I do."

"And do you remember when you said the Norns could see things -- like visions of the future and stuff?"

171

"Yes." Ull obviously had no idea where I was heading.

"Um, well. You don't think it's weird that they can do that? Have visions? See things?"

"No." Ull looked surprised. "Why would that be weird?"

"Because it's not normal -- at least, it's not normal here."

Ull shrugged. "Things are different in Asgard, I guess. We all have our gifts there -- roles we were born to fill. I was born to be a warrior -- the titled god thing just sort of happened. Norns are born to have visions that will allow them to foresee the future. It is a useful gift." He paused. "It's all very structured, but it is the Asgardian way. I suppose that sounds odd to a human."

"Not really." I sipped at my tea to buy myself one more minute. Ull waited patiently, but I could see his foot jiggling under the blanket. Well, I was nervous too. "I mean, I don't think it's weird they can see things because…" I dropped my head and stared at my hands. "Because I can see things too."

13. HISTORY

"PARDON?" ULL GENTLY LIFTED my chin with one finger, forcing me to look into his eyes.

"I can see things." I cringed. "The future. Sometimes the past. Apparently some deranged Elf Man who wants me dead. I see things all the time -- it's like my brain just shuts down and goes into this different world, and sometimes the world looks a whole lot like your world. Last night this insane Elf dragged me to Ýdalir and tried to kill me, but my necklace shot light at him. He just disappeared and I don't know what happened to him.

"Another time, I was standing in this field with you and I was ready to fight these awful monsters that were coming to kill us. Wait," I added hurriedly when I saw the alarmed expression on Ull's face. "I don't just see bad stuff. Sometimes I see good things too -- like this really pretty meadow and a pond with swans and a willow tree with silver leaves." Ull forced a neutral expression, but only after I'd caught a glimpse of fear. I covered my face. "Do you think I'm crazy?"

I expected him to say something right away, but the room was deafening in its silence. I peeked from between my fingers -- Ull was sitting still as a statue, staring into the distance with that forced look of calm. "Oh my God. You're going to dump me." I shouldn't have told him.

Ull shook himself. "Kristia, please. I am not going to dump you." He gently tugged my hands away from my face and pulled me into his chest. "To answer your question, no, sweetheart. I do not think you are crazy. I think you have a very special gift -- in Asgard, sight like yours would qualify you to become a Norn."

"I don't want to be a Norn. I just want to be normal. I hate my visions -- they've kept me outside of everything my whole life, and I just want them to stop."

"But they make you who you are, Kristia. And who knows, maybe you were given this gift for a purpose."

"Yeah, right. So I could *never* fit in, anywhere?"

"You fit with me." Ull stroked my back gently. "My love, I want you to tell me when you see these things. I do not like knowing that someone is frightening you, even if it is only in dreams. I am not entirely sure what to make of that..."

"You could write me off as a fruitcake."

"I happen to like fruitcake." Ull kissed the top of my head. I tilted my face up hopefully and he laughed. "Kristia, be good."

"Fine," I harrumphed. "You're really not going to dump me because you think I'm crazy?"

"Who said I do not think you are crazy?" Ull ducked as I swatted at him. "No, my darling, I am not going anywhere. I am afraid you are stuck with me for as long as you want me."

"Good. Forever, then." I snuggled in closer, practically wilting in relief.

"Forever."

****

With each flip of my "Water Fowl Of The Week" desk calendar, I grew closer to Inga. I could go to her with just about anything and she never judged me. Since I couldn't exactly share Ull's secret with my human friends, Inga was the only one I could talk to about dating a god. She didn't completely understand -- she'd fallen in love with Gunnar as a goddess in her own right -- but she was a good listener. And at least she knew the whole truth.

One afternoon, I showed up at Inga's house with full hands. Ull planted a light kiss on my cheek before he and Gunnar darted out to the driving range to blow off some midterm-exam steam. Inga swept in, gracefully taking my contraband.

"Hello, mortal." her grin was infectious.

"Hello, goddess," I teased back.

"Earl Grey and a Latte?" She nodded to the cups.

"Correct." I dug in my bag and pulled out a grease-spotted package. "And this…" Inga's eyes lit up at the sinful smell.

"Cupcakes!" Her squeal filled the room like a hundred bells. I could never get used to the ethereal sound. "Puff Pastries is my favorite bakery!"

"I know. I figured we could use reinforcements." Our boy-free afternoon involved a marathon of terrible reality shows. So long as we were rotting our minds, we might as well throw in our teeth for good measure.

"Thanks!" Inga traveled to the kitchen so quickly, her gold tunic flew behind her thin frame. She returned in the same movement, with the cupcakes arranged on a square plate. Her trip had taken less than two seconds.

"Inga? What was that?"

"Oh. Are we still supposed to be acting human in front of you? Sorry." Inga sat with deliberate slowness.

I had to laugh. "So you guys are fast?"

"Well I'm faster than most. Especially for a non-titled goddess. The Titleds get extra abilities."

"You don't have a title?" I hoped it wasn't tacky to ask.

"Nope. Oversight on Odin's part, I like to say."

"Why's that?"

"Because, Kristia. *Obviously* I'm supposed to have a title."

"And what title would that be?"

"Domestic Goddess."

"Naturally." I had to smile.

We settled into the deep couch, sipping our drinks and eyeing the cakes. When I spotted a framed photo on the mantel, I realized I didn't know how my new friends had gotten together. "When did you know Gunnar was *the one*?"

"No beating around the bush today. Forever on the brain?" I reddened -- if she only knew. "Well," Inga sipped at her latte, "I knew a lot earlier than he did, I think. We were best friends in school. He was the only one who was any sort of a challenge at fencing. 'Course, I still beat him." She smiled at the memory. "As we grew up, I fell for his naughty sense of humor. And it didn't hurt that he became one of Asgard's best warriors. So when that giant carried me off--" she waved a hand. "Oh honey, don't look so freaked out. Happens all the time. So when the giant showed up, Gunnar came to my rescue. I think that's when it clicked for him, and it wasn't long before I was off the market." Her expression was angelic.

"What about Ull?"

"Well he's lovely, of course, but far too sensitive for me."

"No, I mean when did you meet Ull?"

"Oh," she laughed. "Sorry! He joined our class when his mom married Thor. Poor guy. It had to be hard to move in with the scariest god. And our classmates were tough on Ull because he was so different. He was bigger than the rest of us, and shy. Gunnar took Ull's side, picked him for partners on school projects. Of course, Ull's temper saved Gunnar from more fights than he wants to remember. So... our pair became a threesome, and we've been that way since."

"Ull has a temper?"

"Oh, yes." Inga nodded seriously. "It's mostly under control now but in a fight he's the last one you want to be pitted against."

I mulled that one over. "Thor is scary?"

"At first. He's actually pretty nice if you get to know him. When we were kids, we'd just see the giant hammer and run." She eyed my necklace. "That's Mjölnir at your neck, isn't it?"

I nodded. "It was my grandmother's. She always told me stories about the gods -- myths, I thought back then. I can't believe they turned out to be true."

"You wouldn't believe the stories that are actually true."

"Speaking of that... I hope this isn't inappropriate, but can I ask you something? It's about Ragnarok."

"Okay." Inga was guarded. "But you know Ull doesn't want me scaring you off."

"Trust me, I've had more than enough reasons to be scared off." Not the least of which was the deranged Elf Man. "If I was going anywhere, I'd have left by now."

"Well, all right then. Go ahead."

I took a sip of tea. "Well, it's just… why do all my textbooks and the Internet say that Ragnarok happened, like, forever ago, when you guys talk about it like it's still hanging over your heads?"

"Ull talked to you about Ragnarok?" Inga looked surprised.

"Not exactly. But he alludes to these people wanting his family dead and this dark future and all. I'm assuming he means Ragnarok."

"Well, you assume right. And Ragnarok hasn't happened yet. It's coming, and most likely sooner than later."

"But the Internet says--"

"Oh, Kristia. Do you believe everything you read on the Internet?"

"No." Kind of.

"We wrote those stories ourselves. Somebody, probably a jotun or a dark elf or some other troll, spilled to the humans about this battle that was going to destroy the realms. Naturally, the humans overreacted. We had to come along and clean up the whole mess, which we did by rewriting the stories to look like the battle had already happened and the existing humans were offspring of the survivors." Inga bit into a cupcake. "Mortals are so dramatic. They'd have killed each other off in their panic, if we hadn't stopped them. They gobbled up our little 'myths' -- anything to tell themselves they were safe."

"So Ragnarok hasn't happened yet?"

"Nope."

"And that means..."

"It means it's still going to happen. Eventually. But we don't know when and it's not worth worrying about. Now, can I ask you a question?"

"Of course."

"Good. Back to your necklace." Inga reached out to touch it. When her fingers brushed the cold silver, she recoiled as if she'd been shocked. Reaching out again, she held the charm gently. A look of reverence crossed her face.

"Kristia," she breathed. "You said this was your grandmother's. Do you know where she got it?"

That was weird. "Um... she said one of her relatives got it from a woman in her village named..." I searched my memory. "Ellie? Ellie Norna, I think."

"Elsker! That sneaky Norn!" Inga laughed, a beautiful tinkling sound. "She's the same rogue Norn who told Ull he'd meet you at Cardiff. She's been plotting to get you together for longer than I thought. Kristia, your necklace is elfin made! It was a treasure of Asgard that disappeared years and years ago! Boy, I'll bet Ull had a *look* on his face when he saw it. The love of his life he never wanted to meet, wearing stolen Asgardian property!" Her laughter rang throughout the flat. "Ull really didn't tell you about this?" She rolled her eyes. "He is so determined to protect you from everything."

I shook my head, alarmed. "I swear I didn't steal it. My grandmother gave it to me!"

This only made Inga laugh harder. "Try telling that to Odin!" This couldn't be happening. I could feel the anxiety working its way up. "No, no, Kristia. He won't be mad at you. I'm sure Elsker had her reasons. It's just that Odin's spent hundreds of years wondering where that charm got off to. Its mate is in a museum in London -- a silver charm with his mark, about the size of your hammer. Odin will probably think it's cute when Ull turns up with the missing Mjölnir around his human girlfriend's neck." She collapsed in a fit of laughter.

I wasn't so sure Odin would be amused with the stolen necklace or the human girlfriend, but it was more than I wanted to worry about right then. "Why did you and Gunnar come to Earth?" When in doubt, deflect.

"Because Ull asked us to." It was that simple. "There's very little we wouldn't do for each other. And speaking of Ull," Inga tucked her legs under her as she leaned back into the cushions, "Are you at all anxious about dating a god? We're not exactly light on the baggage -- Ull especially.

You're the first girl he's ever let himself get close to you know. Goddess *or* mortal."

"Well..." It wasn't like I could talk to Ardis or Emma about this. Inga was the only girl on Earth I could actually be honest with. "It's overwhelming sometimes. I mean, Ull is perfect. He's so smart, so thoughtful -- I actually saw him stop traffic once to help an old lady cross the street. He dotes on Olaug; he's ridiculously hot, and he's got this antiquated sense of decency. I mean he has *never, ever* done anything remotely inappropriate with me. Ever. He's just..." What more could I say? "I'm kind of scared I'm not good enough for him."

"Oh Kristia, stop that. You *are* good enough for Ull. You're smart enough to earn a spot at Wales' top university. You're a wonderful friend to me -- and I've never had a human friend. And you're strong in your own way; you've taken all of this in stride and never once complained."

"But he deserves so much more. I'm no goddess."

Inga's eyes softened. "True. But you've done something no goddess could. You softened Ull's heart."

I looked up tentatively.

"Listen, I've known Ull for a long time. He's the headstrong, overbearing brother I never knew I wanted. And for as long as I've known him, Ull's biggest fear has been losing the people he loves. It's why he closed his heart the day we learned Asgard was fated to fall."

"What are you talking about?"

"When a class reaches a certain age, Odin comes to talk about Ragnarok." Inga's eyes clouded over. "Odin tells a room full of children they are all destined to die for the greater good of humankind. It's devastating news, but most of us figure Ragnarok is too far in the future to worry about. Not Ull -- he never got past knowing he was marked and he refused to get close to anyone but Gunnar and I. He didn't want to develop relationships he knew would end. I think it came from losing his birth father at such a young age. So Gunnar and I went on to fall in love and get married. And Ull never dated anyone. Ever. He had lots of chances, but he wouldn't let anyone in."

"That's awful." My heart broke for the boy who'd been too young to learn his fate. I was more grateful than ever for Inga, Gunnar, and Olaug -- without them, Ull would have spent his life completely alone.

"But now he has you," Inga said simply. "And you complement our trio perfectly. It's almost as if you were born to be one of us. Well," she paused, "maybe you were."

"Um, yeah. I was born to be a god."

"It's not impossible, Kristia," Inga said with disdain before her hands flew to her face.

"What do you mean?"

"Oh, no. Ull would kill me. I'm not supposed to talk to you about this."

"Inga, my immortal boyfriend is threatening to give up his godliness to live a human life with me, ending any chance he could have of defending himself at Ragnarok. If you know of another way, you have to tell me."

"Oh…. shoot. Okay. But you cannot tell Ull I'm the one who told you."

I held up my hand. "Girl Scout's Honor."

Inga took a deep breath before blurting out, "Ull doesn't have to become a human for you to be together. You can become a god."

A piece of cupcake lodged in my throat and I coughed trying to free it. I'd pictured as much in my most recent Ragnarok nightmare, but I thought it was just a dream. "That's not possible. Odin would never let a human become a god. Ull said he already asked your dad."

Inga shook her head vehemently. "Ull didn't tell you the whole story. Dad also told him a god once defected to be with a mortal, so Dad and Odin put together a test for a human to become a god. There was no way Odin was going to lose another warrior before Ragnarok, even if it meant letting a human into Asgard."

I held my breath as she continued. "The test is simple. First, a god must choose a human for his wife. Second, Balder must judge the human worthy of the title Protector of Asgard. Third, the human must relinquish her mortality. The formula's been in place for centuries, but nobody knows about it. I figure Dad only told me because he knew your boyfriend would be too stubborn to invite you." She shook her head at my expression. "Oh come on, do you really think Odin would let Ull go so easily? He'd much

rather let you in than lose his best warrior. You watch --
before this plays out you'll be one of us." My head spun as
she finished. "Kristia Tostenson, you are, plainly, the only
human in the history of mankind who has a shot at
becoming a god!"

****

I wish I could say I handled the news in stride. I spent
the better part of that night staring at my ceiling, actively
seeking its imperfections to avoid thinking about what I'd
learned. When I'd discovered every crack and dimple, I
moved on to scouring the walls, then counted the leaves of
the tree outside my window. By the time I'd reached three
hundred, seventy-four, I was no closer to sleep and had to
accept the futility of my exercise. I gave my mind over to
the obsession it had avoided all day and waited for the panic
attack to come.

My stomach churned like a blade at a cheese factory
while I replayed Inga's words in my head. A shot at
becoming a god. How was that even possible? I slowly
worked through the ramifications. *Superhuman abilities, Ull's
equal in every way.* That sounded pretty nice. *A life marked for
death, unimaginable responsibilities.* Not so good.

I'd never really thought about my death, what with my
being twenty and healthy. And I wasn't so keen on the idea
of dying at the hands of some bloodthirsty monster or
being hauled off by a giant like Inga. *Divine status, the power to*

control the elements. My limited imagination had barely let me play dress-up with Ardis when we were kids; I'd certainly never seen myself becoming immortal. *Prejudiced Asgardians, knowing I would always be inferior.* That was a hard one.

I already had something of a complex -- I wasn't the prettiest, the smartest, or the most coordinated among humans. How would I fare as a god? *Ageless beauty, strength and grace.* Well, that would certainly help with the inferiority complex. *Leaving my family behind, losing my mortality.* My throat swelled. Was I really willing to give up my parents and Ardis? And my mortality... was I really ready to end my life at twenty?

True, it hadn't been much of a life before Ull came into it. But I didn't know the first thing about being an immortal. How could I possibly commit to it for an eternity? *An eternity with Ull.* My mind stopped. An eternity with Ull. That was all I wanted. Unending time with the man I loved. Whatever the costs, whatever the losses, would any of it matter as long as we were together?

My decision was made before I realized I had committed. I doubt it had ever been in question. Whatever the fallout, if he asked me to spend my life with him, I would be at Ull's side. As a god.

****

Once I'd made up my mind, it was surprisingly easy to

avoid thinking about giving up my mortality. I kept my decision to myself, and thankfully Inga didn't bring it up. As the semester drew to a close, I looked forward to my two uninterrupted weeks with Ull. Though we'd been virtually inseparable at Cardiff, I never felt like I could have enough time with him. Classes kept us apart for chunks of the day and he'd leave my flat much too early at night, presumably to give me the chance to finish studying. Emma and Victoria loved to tease me about his constant presence in our apartment whenever I wasn't at his, and I knew there would be plenty of heckling as I said goodbye to the girls for the holiday.

St. Lucia's Day dawned clear and crisp, and I helped Victoria and Emma pack their suitcases for their trips home.

"Happy Christmas!" Emma sang out, jubilant at the freedom vacation brought.

"Yes, Happy Christmas," Victoria echoed slyly. "Have a wonderful time with your man. Don't do anything I wouldn't do…"

"So pretty much do anything you want!" Emma ribbed. Victoria threw a pillow at her. "What? You know it's true."

Shrugging, Victoria conceded. "It's true. Enjoy your holiday."

"It's really not like that. I swear." But my protest fell on deaf ears.

"Yes, I'm sure you've been spending months with that

spectacular specimen and all you're doing is studying." Victoria snickered. Emma chuckled, amused by my blush.

I wished they were right. Despite my saucy dream and my pitiful advances, some archaic code of chivalry prevented Ull from doing anything he considered 'inappropriate'. I was really hoping that two weeks together would weaken his resolve. Did that make me easy? I giggled, knowing I was probably the last person that term could ever apply to. Ardis always said that I was pure as the driven snow -- a label I hated. But who could look at any of the boys from Nehalem without remembering them pulling wings off flies and eating worms? I'd had dates to prom and homecoming of course, but it went without saying, my romantic history was pretty limited.

"Trust me, if anything exciting happens, you'll be the first to know. Now go home. Have a great holiday." The girls hooted and hollered all the way to Victoria's car.

With my friends safely off to see their families, I was left at loose ends. I triple checked the contents of my suitcase against my packing list and was going back a fourth time when Ull appeared at the door. I rushed to it, eagerly bringing my bag with me. He pulled me close, then leaned back to give me a look that made me flush.

"Is this outfit appropriate to watch my Norse-god boyfriend's Norse-goddess friend play Saint Lucia at the Norse church?" I twirled, to Ull's amused smile.

"You look beautiful, Kristia." He leaned in to smell my hair. "Just like always." I blushed again and Ull escorted me to his car.

At the church, we saw twinkling, white lights strung around the roses in the garden and garlands hanging over each entrance. We walked through the courtyard, pausing at the stone bench where Ull had first opened up to me. So much had happened since then, it was hard to remember the time when I'd thought Ull was gone from my life forever. I grimaced -- hard, but not impossible. I pushed the memory away and focused on the man standing in front of me. As always, looking at Ull took my breath away. He pulled me to his chest, holding me tightly before gently guiding me into the warm building.

Inside, the atmosphere was festive. Our tiny church was absolutely filled with St. Lucia's day revelers, and we hurried to fill the last two seats in the pew where Gunnar was waiting.

"That's my girl," came Gunnar's proud whisper. A hush fell over the group as Inga led a procession of young girls up the aisle. They were dressed in simple white robes with garlands on top of their heads, and they held lit candles in their hands. Inga's robe was tied with a crimson sash and her evergreen crown held a wreath of candles, actual lit candles. I would have set the church on fire in ten seconds flat if I wore a flaming headdress, but Inga walked so gracefully I wanted to cry. She was so beautiful, her pale hair shining in the candlelight. I snuck a look at Gunnar, who was beaming with pride. Inga winked sweetly at her husband, gliding up the aisle trailed by little angels. At the front, the girls sang a song in Norwegian as Inga smiled seraphically throughout. The pastor gave a blessing, a handful of women in their bunads gave readings, and Inga glided back up the aisle, trailed by her choir of cherubs.

Ull squeezed my shoulders lightly as the last notes resonated through the room. I leaned into his tall frame and inhaled his delicious scent. The worshippers stood, chatting familiarly. Thousands of miles from home, I had found a community every bit as tightly-knit as Nehalem. I had found friends who accepted me, in spite of astronomical differences. I had a wonderful guy who, for some unfathomable reason, adored me beyond the bounds of logic. Sitting very still, I relished the peace emanating from my core, the deep happiness I'd only known since meeting Ull Myhr. Nestled under his arm, I'd found my happy place.

14. THE PROPOSAL

IT WAS DARK WHEN we pulled up the tree-lined driveway of Ýdalir, crunching tires on gravel the only sound I heard. Ull stepped out of the Range Rover, yawning in an uncharacteristic display of exhaustion. He'd been more tired than usual over the past few weeks, probably from worrying about the end-of-the-cosmos battle he was loathe to talk about. I knew he didn't want to scare me, but my fate was so tied to his that anxiety was unavoidable. I couldn't imagine a world without him and I wished he would open up. If nothing else, I could be a shoulder to… well, talk on. The idea of Ull crying was ridiculous.

Ull carried our suitcases into the house, depositing mine in the guest room. I'd been hoping for some impropriety, but I knew better than to expect anything of the sort. I should have been grateful. Compared to a goddess, I was sure to be a disappointment, so the less experienced he was the better I'd look. On the other hand, Ull, in all his physical perfection, had waited an eternity to be with anyone. I seriously doubted I'd prove worth waiting for.

My thoughts were interrupted by his husky voice inviting me to join him on the terrace. I hurriedly ran a brush through my hair and raced through the living room. I didn't want to waste another minute away from him. Outside, I skidded to a stop while my vision adjusted to the night. "Ull?"

I found him standing beneath the yew dale. He smiled expectantly, holding out one hand in welcome. I locked my eyes on his before staring at the ground. It was so familiar. A circle of candles framed the grass where he waited. They marked a path along the cobblestone walkway, rounding the English roses, leading to where I stood. Thousands of twinkling lights hung from the trees and more candles stood in hurricane glasses along the stone wall.

It was all so carefully arranged. The lights in the trees winked down at me like the stars overhead. Looking up, I remembered another night, dancing under the stars at my high school's homecoming dance. It had been freezing cold. My date was one of the three Mikes in our class, and he'd been a little too handsy. I'd feigned a need for the powder room and found Ardis hiding in there too. We'd run away from our dud dates, sitting on the football field in our fancy dresses and complaining about how dismal our dating prospects were in such a tiny town. Would we ever meet anyone worthy of our wonderfulness?

I looked to the row of flickering candles in glasses along the wall. My mind moved to another memory, a bonfire on the beach after exams my freshman year at UPN. My platonic lab partner with questionable breath sat next to me on a thick driftwood log, squirming anxiously until he turned to plant an unwanted kiss squarely on my lips. Thankfully I'd had a rare moment of grace, reaching to pick up a rock at just the right moment so the poor guy dove headfirst into the sand. Would my Prince Charming ever show up?

My eyes scanned the garden again, taking in the twinkling lights, the candles framing the tree, and the man standing in the middle of it all, his hand stretched out waiting for me to join him. How had my life gone from pawsy, high school boys in a one-light town to this? I took a tentative step towards Ull and looked around again. The yard was well decorated, even for Ýdalir. Could this be what I thought it was?

Everything clicked into slow motion as I realized what was happening. I made my way forward, carefully placing each foot in front of the other, sure I was going to trip over myself. I was hyper-aware of the cool, English night, the whoosh of a nearby owl taking flight, the sound of the small stones beneath my feet. I zeroed in on the glow from Ull's brilliant eyes.

I made my way to my future, pausing breathlessly before the standing form of my real-life Nordic hero. He reached out to take both of my hands in his, the brilliant white smile never leaving his face. He squeezed my fingers. I breathed in and out, trying to commit every detail of this moment to memory.

"Kristia Tostenson," Ull began in his velvety voice, making my knees weak. "You have changed my life beyond measure. In all my years, I never knew I could feel so peaceful, so at home. I have searched the realms for a place to belong, never seeing it was you I should have been searching for. I am home wherever you are. Where your heart is, mine is at peace. You are my everything."

He dropped to one knee and drew in an uneven breath. The corner of his mouth twitched in a nervous half-smile and he rubbed his palms together. My heart thudded and I stopped breathing when Ull reached behind his back to retrieve a small, dark box. His hand shook as he opened it, revealing a circle of diamonds exquisite in their simplicity. "Kristia." His voice caught. "I pledge to love you for the rest of my existence. I will protect you and provide you with the happiest home you have ever known. Please do me the honor of becoming my wife. Will you have me as your husband?"

I was too overwhelmed to answer. This was a destiny I'd never have imagined in Nehalem. Ull had chosen *me*, simple Kristia Tostenson from a one-stoplight town. It was beyond belief. I knew what I was going to have to do if I wanted to be a part of his life -- become a god, leave my life behind. I was going to have to give up everything I'd ever known. But I'd made my mind up weeks ago, when faced with the decision of whether to choose Ull or choose everything else, there was no contest. I would always choose Ull.

When I finally found my voice it was strong. "Yes. I want to be by your side. Always." He wrapped me in a tremendous embrace and swept me off my feet, spinning me until we fell.

Ull propped himself up on an elbow and brushed a

strand of hair from my face. He lowered his body so it hovered over mine and pressed his lips to my own. A hesitant kiss at first, as if he were seeking permission. A slow burn built and his kiss became less tentative, more urgent. His hand trailed down my ribs and I grabbed at his hair, pulling him closer. I was overwhelmed by the sensation of his touch, the heat of his lips, and the indescribable electricity flowing between us.

I wrapped my leg around his hip, pulling him on top of me. He groaned -- it must have been too much. He broke our embrace by rolling onto his back. We lay side by side, staring up at the tree.

"I hope you want a short engagement, my love. I need to make you my wife as soon as possible."

"That sounds good to me." I rolled to my side so I could look at him.

"Shall we marry after graduation? Are your parents coming to Wales then?"

I nodded. "And Ardis too." It would be the perfect time -- and in just five months. I hated waiting for anything. There was no way I had the patience to be engaged for longer than that.

"Wait," Ull stood and walked behind the tree. He came back with a silver ice bucket holding a bottle and two glasses. Uncorking the champagne, he filled the glasses and handed me one. I sniffed at it.

"I can't drink this. I'm underage." I was not about to

abandon a lifetime of following the rules just because I was engaged.

"Kristia, we are in the UK. The drinking age here is eighteen. But it is up to you -- I have sparkling water in the house if you prefer." My eyes lit up. I hadn't realized the law was different. In that case, I couldn't think of a better excuse for champagne than my engagement to Ull. I eagerly raised my glass. "Skål." Ull smiled.

"Cheers," I said back, taking a sip. The bubbles tickled my throat.

"You really want to marry me?" Ull seemed uncertain.

"Oh, yes," I breathed. "I do. You're the most amazing thing that has ever happened to me. I had no idea life could be like... well, like this." I gestured to the beauty around us.

"This is only the beginning." Ull smiled happily. "Wait until you see where we spend our honeymoon."

"I thought the bride got to make that decision."

"No, darling. The groom makes that decision. The bride makes all the other decisions." I had to laugh. "So tell me, Miss Tostenson, how have you pictured your wedding day?"

"Truthfully? I never gave it much thought."

"Neither did I." Ull chuckled. "Guess that leaves us with a blank slate."

"Well, if I had to come up with something, I'd want it

to be small. I'd wear my grandmother's dress and carry ivory roses--"

"Why ivory roses?" Ull interrupted.

I felt my cheeks grow warm. "Because they're in your garden."

He smiled. "I like that."

"And I'd want us to dance under the stars. I've never had a romantic dance under the stars before." Just a couple of really uncomfortable ones.

Ull took the glass from my hand and set it beside the dale. He wrapped an arm around my waist and led me in a slow dance. I tried to follow, but ended up smashing his foot.

"Sorry," I mumbled.

"We can work up to steps." Ull pulled me closer and I rested my head on his chest. I could hear his heart beating against my cheek as we swayed back and forth in the moonlight. The cool air caressed my arms as Ull guided me around the candlelit ballroom he'd created. My goose bumps weren't entirely due to the temperature. As the dance ended, he lifted my chin with one finger and kissed me on the lips. "Jeg elsker det, Kristia. Thank you for making me the happiest god alive."

"I love you too, Ull," I whispered. This was the greatest day of my entire life.

****

Back in my room, I could barely hold my hand steady to dial the international code through my mobile phone. I kept staring at the sparkling ring on my left hand. But the day would not be complete without this phone call, and I willed myself to dial. When the familiar voice answered, I let out the quietest squeal my excitement would allow. "Ardis, I'm getting married!"

The scream that met my ear wasn't nearly so soft, and I had to pull the phone away to protect what was left of my hearing. "Oh my god, oh my god, when? Where? To Ull? See, I told you it would work out! His parents love you!"

"Well…" I bit my lip. His parents had slipped my mind. "They haven't met me yet. But I think they'll be okay." Would they? I tried not to think about it. Tonight was for celebrating.

"Oh my god, Kristia. You're getting married! So things are going good," Ardis teased.

"Things are great! We're at his country house--"

"Again? Get on with your bad self, sistah!" I didn't have the heart to crush her inflated opinion of me, so I didn't mention our sleeping arrangements. "How did he ask? What does the ring look like? Oh Kristia, I can't believe this is happening!"

"I can't believe it either. I always thought you'd be the first one to get married."

"Are you kidding me? There are way too many guys out there for me to pick just one. Yet." Her giggles filled me with happiness.

"Oh, Ardis, I miss you!"

"I miss you too! Now tell me how he proposed!"

I settled back into the overstuffed pillows, recounting almost every detail of my perfect evening.

"Is he seriously as hot as you say he is? Or are you exaggerating? C'mon Kristia, he can't really be that sexy. He's in England." I had to laugh at Ardis' reasoning. She was my best friend in the world. Gosh how I missed her.

I could not wait to introduce her to Ull.

****

A few days later, I woke up in a cold sweat. My nightmare had been so real, I couldn't be sure this one wasn't a vision. I reminded myself that my visions had never been particularly useful, so this must have been a dream. Ull had gotten a phone call and escaped to his study so I wouldn't hear.

"Ja," he'd answered anxiously.

"Ull, it is happening. The Norns have foreseen Balder's death. It will happen before the snow melts from the mountains -- it will be this spring." Olaug's voice crackled through the mobile phone in Norwegian, but somehow I understood all the words. Ull collapsed onto his leather chair.

"It cannot be so soon. It cannot happen in Kristia's lifetime."

"I am sorry Ull. Ragnarok is beginning. The giants and dark elves have begun to move together, someone is already organizing the attack. All that is left is for Balder to die -- it will give our enemies the opening they need to start this fight. It will happen within five months."

"Ragnarok." Ull dropped the phone and closed his eyes, silent tears falling as I woke up in a panic.

15. RAGNAROK

I SHOULD HAVE TOLD Ull about my dream the minute I woke up, but I just couldn't bring myself to do it.

"God morgen," Ull greeted me in the kitchen. He stood at the stove wearing a thick sweater and wielding a spatula. "Have a seat." He kissed me softly and gestured to the stool at the island.

"Pancakes today? Yum." I was famished.

"You will need your energy. We are taking a hike."

"Where to today?"

"I want to show you my favorite plants in Bibury. And the willows off the Coln are a good couple of miles from here." He was so relaxed. It didn't seem right to kill the mood by telling him we were all going to die within months. I could break the news over lunch.

Of course, I didn't manage to do that either. This wasn't the sort of news that should be shared over food. I could tell him right before tea time. And I wouldn't think about it until then.

But three hours later, we sat with steaming mugs and I still hadn't shared my dream. *Coward.*

"I win," I gloated. I took a sip of tea as I captured Ull's last checker.

"Again," Ull muttered. My betrothed was surprisingly bad at board games. Petty as it was, I was pleased to find one thing I could do better than him.

A low buzzing broke his focus, and he eyed the ringing mobile. I was immobilized by sudden terror. "I apologize, darling." he kissed my clammy forehead. "I will only be a minute." And he darted into the study speaking hurriedly in Norwegian. It was hot when he did that, but for once I was too horrified to notice. "Ja?" I heard him say. Oh, no, no, no. Crimeney, no. I was too late to warn him.

I crept towards the study, not wanting him to know I was eavesdropping. I heard him collapse into the leather chair. "It cannot be so soon," he whispered. "It cannot happen in Kristia's lifetime." I clapped both hands over my mouth. Ull was silent for a long time, and when he finally spoke his voice was filled with dread. "Ragnarok."

I walked to the kitchen, adrenaline pulsing. Why hadn't I said something sooner? I should have warned him this call was coming. And what was happening to my normally hapless visions? Where were the toenail painting and the laundry folding? That scene played out exactly the way it had in my dream. Oh my God, Ragnarok was coming. And my visions were giving me a front row seat.

I waited for Ull to come out of his study, but he stayed put. I puttered around the kitchen, appreciating that Olaug left the fridge and pantry well stocked in her absence. Guilt made me hungry. I took out the pitcher of waffle batter and was looking for Ull's favorite jam in the pantry when I heard him collapse on the couch. I eyed him warily. He'd asked me to tell him about my visions, and I'd been too chicken. Would he want to know that I knew? Or should I let him tell me in his own time?

"Who was that?" My voice was so high he should have seen right through me.

"Uh, it was Gunnar." His eyes darted back and forth, thick worry lines between his brows giving him away. "He wanted to say Happy Christmas."

"Is that all?"

Ull balled his fists and tried to look calm. "That's all." He was trying so hard to protect me. I couldn't let him suffer anything else on his own.

"Ull, I know. I know it was Olaug and that Balder's going to die. I know Ragnarok is coming." I wiped my palms on my pants.

"Were you eavesdropping? Wait, even if you were, how would you know that? Olaug used Norwegian. Do you speak Norwegian now too?"

I grimaced. "No more than yesterday. I just... ugh, I'm a huge coward. I'm sorry, I should have told you this morning. But you were so happy, and we were having such a nice time, I didn't want to bring you down. I'll be more honest about what I see, I swear I will. I just couldn't upset you. I'm so sorry--"

"Kristia, slow down. What are you talking about?"

"I had a dream last night. Or a vision, I guess. It's hard to tell what's what anymore. Olaug called, she told you Ragnarok was starting. Real soon." With all I'd learned in the past few months, I should have known that it would come true in my lifetime -- the stories Mormor told me, the nightmares I'd had ever since. The battle that would end our worlds. Oh my God, this was really happening. I rubbed at my temples.

Ull shook his head. "I tried never to speak of Ragnarok -- I did not want you to worry."

"Not worry? Ull, we met in Mythology Class. Professor Carnicke talked about Ragnarok the first day of school. You told me you had a dark future. And you told me you're a god. Between what I already knew and what I picked up from a quick Google search, I know *all* about Ragnarok." I crossed to the couch and knelt beside him. "It's the digital age -- not Viking times."

"I apologize Kristia. I only wanted to protect you."

"You're going to have to start trusting me sometime."

"I know." Ull rubbed his forehead.

"And Ull." I lifted his chin until he met my eyes. "You don't have to die. You know that, right?" Granted, the Internet was more than clear on what was going to happen to most of the gods and the earth come Ragnarok, but Inga swore that was all hearsay -- fabrications by Asgardians to protect insecure humans. I was choosing to believe Inga. "You don't have to let some silly prophecy run your life. You can do that for yourself."

"Even gods cannot escape the fates." Ull shook his head sadly. "In theory the future can change. But the Norns have prophesied our fall at Ragnarok for as long as I have been alive. Nothing has ever altered it. And I doubt anything can."

He looked so hopeless. I sat next to my morose idol on the couch, wishing more than anything that there was something I could do. "Ull," I laid my head on his shoulder, "you do have some control here. You can fight. You don't have to resign yourself to this awful future just because some Norns said so. I don't understand how can you just accept their word as law."

"You wouldn't." His eyes filled with a hundred lifetimes of sorrow. "Because it is so different for mortals. But for us, their predictions become truths. I wish it were otherwise."

He really believed all this prophecy stuff. "Oh Ull." There was nothing else to say. Ull rested his head on mine.

"I thought we had more time. I thought we could live out our human lives, grow old, pass on, long before any of this came to be." He was despondent. "I cannot protect you after all. I am so sorry, Kristia." Oh, crumbs on a cracker. Ull was crying. His silent tears fell onto my cheek, and I pressed my hand to the chest of the deity whose greatest fear was coming true. I couldn't let him face this. There was one thing I could do. Ull would not lose one more person he loved.

"Listen, I know something else too. I know you aren't going to become a human. Not for me." His body was crumpled in defeat. Shaking my head, I voiced my decision. The decision I'd made weeks ago, that same night Inga had told me it was an option. "Listen to me. I want to be like you. I want to be Goddess of Winter. I want to fight for your family -- and for you."

Ull's sharp breath was equaled in severity only by the anger in his eyes. I shouldn't have known about this option. "Absolutely not. Ragnarok is not a joke, Kristia, and it is coming. I will not let you die for me."

"I won't die." I wasn't being stubborn; I really believed my words. "None of us will. Ull, I know I can do this. If I'm with you, then Ragnarok will end without the loss of a single Asgardian life."

Ull's patronizing look made it clear he was unconvinced. "Kristia, darling. You do not know what you are talking about. The Three Sisters have predicted our fall at Ragnarok since the beginning of time. Very little escapes their visions."

"Maybe. But they never saw me coming. Elsker never got to tell them about me, remember? So maybe their prophecy would have changed if they'd known what I can do."

"I do not follow."

"You said yourself, my visions are a gift. That I'd qualify to be a Norn if I'd been born like you. So if I can see things, predict what your enemies are going to do… and if they don't even know I exist because of this prophecy…" He still wasn't following. "Ull. Use me! Make me a goddess and let me use my visions to help. I'll be like an undercover agent. Your enemies won't be expecting me since no human has ever become a god. Nobody but Jens and Odin even knew it was an option." The fury in Ull's eyes blazed as he realized it was Inga who had told me too much about his world.

The choices he'd never wanted me to have lay in front of him, and he had no control over my decision. The path to joining his realm was clear. And immediate. Under Odin's test to become a god, only Balder could judge my worthiness, and he would have to do that before someone killed him. Surely Ull knew all of this, and he was beyond angry that I did too.

"You do not know what you are saying. Kristia, if you become a goddess then at Ragnarok, our fates are entwined. You will meet the same end that I will, whatever it may be." I couldn't comprehend the lifetime of sorrow that this prophecy had caused him. No wonder, in his eons of existence, he'd never gotten married. He believed it would be a death sentence for his bride.

"Maybe. But I know a few things you don't."

"Oh really? What exactly do you know?" I could tell Ull wasn't taking me very seriously. My thinly stretched nerves threatened to snap.

"Listen, I know you're going to keep Asgard safe, okay? That you'll imprison whoever is controlling these giants and elves and whatever else is trying to kill us. That you're going to use magic to trap the perp in some silvery bubble so he can't hurt us again." I'd seen as much last week. At the time I thought it was another dream, but recent events made it clear I had to start taking my dreams a lot more seriously.

"How could you possibly know about the Asgardian prison cell? Or about my magic?"

"Wait, you can actually do magic?"

"Don't change the subject."

"Fine. I saw it in another vision. I didn't tell you because I thought it was a dream. Happy?"

"Not even a little. This is getting too dangerous for you. If our enemies find out everything you know about us... and them..." Ull shook his head. "Kristia, I do not want you to change for me. I cannot allow you to tie your fate to mine."

"Oh, please. Like my fate could ever *not* be tied to yours. If you are going to... fall," I choked on the word, "then I want to be with you. You are my life and nothing -- epic battle, death, homicidal giants -- nothing could keep me away from you. I love you," I finished, hoping he understood how true my words were.

"And you would choose..." His eyes studied the floor.

"I would choose to die an Asgardian by your side rather than change a single thing about you. I love you exactly as you are, and I always will."

"Kristia, I cannot allow this."

"I'm sorry, Ull. It's not your choice to make. I'll go to Odin by myself -- you know I will. Inga will take me. And you know he'll let me into Asgard if it means keeping you in his army." Ull's eyes burned. He was furious, whether at Inga or me I wasn't sure.

"You would go behind my back?" His voice was so cold I almost checked the windows for frost.

"If it's the only way to save you, then yes." I defied him.

"How could you do this to me?"

"I'm not doing anything to you. I'm doing this for you."

"I do not want this."

"Tough. It's happening. You made this decision the day you asked to borrow my notes." We stared eye to eye, glaring at each other. I was not going to back down.

Ull's shoulders dropped. "Why are you doing this, Kristia? Why do you insist on doing the exact opposite of everything I ask of you?"

My mouth twitched. "Nobody's ever told you no

before, have they?"

"Not in this realm."

"Well get used to it."

Ull gave me a shaky look. "Kristia, are you certain? Do you have to do this?"

"Absolutely." I declared without hesitation.

"I do not agree with this."

"I do not agree with letting you march off to your death. Guess we're even." We stared at each other. Ull was the first to blink.

"Then we have work to do." He stood in resignation, pulling me gently to him and kissing the top of my head softly. "I do not agree with this," he said again.

"Do you want me to marry you?"

"Of course I do."

"Then get used to making decisions that work for both of us -- not just you."

"This decision does not work for me."

"Fine, then get used to doing things that make your wife happy."

He looked frustrated, but I knew I had gotten my way. He led me to the table and sat me on his knee. Opening his laptop, he began the call he had spent his lifetime hoping he'd never have to make. "God ettermiddag, Olaug," he said despondently to her image on the screen. "Kristia wants in. Will you arrange for a meeting with Odin and Balder?"

"Veldig bra! Ja. I would be honored." Olaug knew what this meant. "Kristia, I do hope Odin gives his consent. You would make a fine goddess." she signed off. I sat for a moment as I processed what I might become.

I smiled bravely. "Do you think he'll say yes?"

"I should say absolutely not. He has never allowed it before -- it goes against everything he stands for. But with my luck," Ull said wryly, "it is not out of the question."

"Good. Ull, you have to trust me. Everything is going to work out." Ull looked unsteady as he faced a reality he'd feared for an eternity. I cupped his perfect face between my hands. Without thinking, I leaned in and kissed him soundly. He started to pull back, but I held his jaw between my palms, forcing our lips to keep contact. He gave in, wrapping both arms tightly around my waist and crushing my torso to his. I lost myself as his arms held me firmly in place and his lips reminded me of how much was at stake. I released my hold on his face and tangled my fingers in his hair, feeling the strands wrap around my engagement ring. His lips were so warm. His breathing grew heavy and he was the first to pull away.

"Kristia, what are you doing to me?" He groaned. "You cannot kiss me like that to get your way."

"I just did." I smiled lazily. "Now listen. I want to be a

211

god. I can do this. I am going to be just fine. Really."

I wasn't sure which of us I was trying to convince.

****

I thought the matter was settled, but as we were cleaning up after dinner, Ull brought it up one final time.

"Kristia, are you absolutely certain you want to tie your fate with mine? I cannot escape Ragnarok, but you may still be able to live a happy life with someone else if we somehow save your realm." The words had to hurt him.

"Oh, quit trying to get rid of me." I dried my hands on a dishtowel. "I'm not living in any world that you're not a part of, so stop trying to save me from a fate I don't want to be saved from. Whatever happens, we fight together. And if it comes to it, we die together. But you," I growled, "are not facing *anything* without me. *Ever.*"

Ull's eyes broke my heart, but he pulled me to him, breathing deeply into my hair. I inhaled the invigorating scent of pine that followed him wherever he went and felt the knotted muscles of his back beneath my palms. "I don't know how to convince you, Ull, but I know, deep down, that Ragnarok will not be the end of your family. You have to trust me." He looked at me questioningly, then kissed my forehead and poured two cups of tea.

"Kristia Tostenson, you are something else." I

remembered a conversation we'd had in the fall.

"Remember when you told me about Elsker? How she told you where to find me?"

"Yes?"

"Well, why did you? Come find me, I mean? According to Inga, you've been following the rules your whole life. Why stop now?"

"Ah." Ull raised his eyebrows. We wandered to the garden with steaming mugs. "That is a good question. I am not entirely sure I know the answer myself. I think I had gotten so lonely that I could not take it anymore. I have always done what Asgard asks of me. A warrior lives a terribly isolating existence. I think I finally got greedy. I started to feel like I deserved my own happiness." He shrugged. "Things are different for Asgardians than they are for humans. Our lives are laid out for us on the day we are born. The Norns foretell our futures and, with very few exceptions, things play out exactly as they say, all in accordance with the law. I was born to be a warrior first, titled god second, to serve my realm over myself. Duty above all -- it is our way."

"That sounds stifling." I couldn't imagine having my life mapped out for me.

"It is. And like I said, I was terribly lonely. When Elsker told me there was someone out there for me, she threw me a lifeline. It was my chance to have what I had always wanted, to not be alone anymore -- even if it did openly defy the law. It took me a while to warm to the idea, but eventually I did. It saved me."

"I'm glad you came around."

"I am too.

"Ull?" Knowing this was shaky ground, I trod lightly. "Do you really believe someone else controls your destiny?"

"The Three Sisters -- yes. Why?"

"Do you ever get sick of that? Of not feeling in charge of your own life?"

"You have no idea." His voice was dark. "But that is how things are. We each have our posts -- some of us are warriors, some control the elements, and some lay out the future. It is our way." He kept saying that. The Asgardian way. "You know, that is part of why I seemed so angry when we first met. I was jealous."

"Jealous?" The God of Winter was jealous of me?

"Yes. Your life is yours to live -- you picked up and moved from Oregon to Wales just because you wanted to."

"You moved from Asgard to Bibury."

"But it is not the same. I must do what is asked of me for the rest of my existence. Even here I am at Odin's beck and call. And you," he stroked my cheek softly, "your destiny is totally in your hands. Of course I was jealous."

An idea was mulling around in my head, an inkling of why Elsker had sent Ull to me instead of to another Asgardian. Maybe she was sick of these Fate ladies controlling everything and she wanted me to show Ull he had the power to make his own destiny. Being human, I had a totally different perspective than any Asgardian. And I think Elsker wanted me to do what no Asgardian girl could do -- show Ull he could buck the system and take charge of his own life.

"Jeg elsker det, Kristia," Ull said, taking hold of my hand.

"I love you too." I lowered my head to his chest, thinking of all he had shouldered. I wished more than anything that I could put his mind at ease. I knew everything was going to work out -- I just had no idea how.

16. JUDGMENT

THE NEXT DAY, ULL was in a considerably lighter mood. "Sweetheart," he kissed my head over breakfast, "We will put up a good fight come Ragnarok. But I do not want to think about it anymore. I just want to enjoy our time in the country while we have it."

"Really? Just like that? Aren't you still upset?" I certainly wouldn't have been able to shut off my worry switch.

"I am fine, darling. Let us not talk about it again."

"Fair enough. What do you want to talk about?"

Ull raised an eyebrow. "How about our wedding?"

"Right. Um, who exactly is coming from your side?"

"Probably just my parents and grandfather. Odin does not like to have too many of us away from Asgard at once."

Now it was my turn to worry. First, I was beyond nervous about meeting Ull's parents. Ull's mom had golden hair -- not hair the color of gold, but hair actually *made* of gold. And Thor was, well, a big deal. The most influential person I'd ever spent time with was the Mayor of Nehalem, and he *had* to be nice to me because he was Ardis' uncle. The rulers of the celestial realm didn't have that obligation.

"Do you think they'll like me? I can't be what they imagined for a daughter-in-law."

"Of course they will like you. Why would you ask?"

"Just wondering." Wondering if they'll like me enough to make me a god. Wondering if I'll be any good at being divine. Wondering what it'll feel like to be changed. That's all.

"Darling, you have nothing to worry about on that front." Yeah, right.

I put my worries aside on Christmas morning. I woke up early and threw my gray ballet sweater on top of the blue pajama pants and tank top I'd worn to bed. The ballet sweater was as close as I would ever get to the graceful dance. I padded in blue, fuzzy slippers toward the smell of apple pastries.

Ull was taking Olaug's tarts out of the oven. I snuck up behind him and wrapped my arms around his waist. He turned with a huge smile and bent to kiss me, his lips hot on mine. I forgot to breathe and my fingers curled into fists against the muscles of his back. He lifted me, drawing me even closer. My need for air won out and I pulled back gasping.

"Am I ever going to get used to this?"

"I hope not." He smiled. "Happy Christmas, darling."

"Mmm..." I snuggled closer, still in his arms. "It is happy." I breathed in his deliciously woodsy scent and tilted my head up. Ull's chiseled jaw was calling to me, and I stretched on my tiptoes to kiss it.

"I have a gift for you." He untangled himself and reached for a small wrapped box on the counter.

"You mean the diamond engagement ring wasn't my Christmas present?"

Ull laughed, the jovial laugh I loved best. "No, love." He handed me a cup of tea and pointed to the living room. Overnight, he'd transformed it into a pacific-northwestern paradise. Real evergreen garlands hung across the mantel and above the French doors. A six-foot tree stood in the corner, decorated with white lights and red, felt ornaments. Each side of the French doors hosted an evergreen wreath and a fire burned in the fireplace, filling the small space with its warmth.

"Do you like it?" Ull squeezed my hand.

"It's perfect. It smells like home." It did. The evergreens took me thousands of miles back to the forests of Oregon, and the aroma coming from the oven reminded me of the apple pies Mormor used to bake with our Christmas supper.

"That was my goal. Happy Christmas, my love." He held the wrapped box out for me.

"Oh! Wait, I have something for you too." I ran to my room and rummaged through my drawer until I came up with my gift. I'd agonized over what to buy Ull, and I was really excited to give it to him. Racing back to the living room, I skidded to a stop in my slippered feet. "Here." I thrust my present into Ull's hands. He laughed at my enthusiasm. He pulled me down so we both sat on the soft rug in front of the fireplace.

"You first," I said. I couldn't wait. He smiled as I bounced on my knees.

"Hmm." He tugged at the bow with excruciating slowness. "It seems to be stuck." He was teasing me and I couldn't take it.

"Oh just open it already!" I lunged for the present intending to rip the wrapping right off, but Ull was too quick. He pulled it out of my reach, and I nearly fell right into his lap. "Hey," I mumbled as I righted myself. "That's not fair." I'd better be more graceful when I was a goddess.

"Sorry, darling, I'll try not to tease you anymore."

"Oh, yeah. Like that'll happen anytime soon."

"True." But he did open the present a little less slowly, shooting teasing glances at me all the while. When he finally got the wrapping paper off, he reached into the box. "A rugby ball. Thank you, darling."

"No, *look* at the ball." He did, and recognition dawned.

He grinned. "Is this--"

"I got the whole National team to sign it!"

"How did you get this?"

"Inga and I waited outside the locker room after a game. She had to point out which guys were the players because I had no clue, and we just asked them all to sign."

"Kristia, this is really thoughtful. I love it." He turned the ball over in his hands. "Wow. Thank you." He reached over to give me a hug. "Nobody has ever done anything like this for me before."

"You deserve it," I said simply. "You're their number one fan."

Ull shook his head. "You are something else, Kristia Tostenson. Now you open yours."

I tugged at the white bow and it slipped off the box. I lifted the lid and inhaled sharply. "Ull," I whispered. "This is too much." Snowflake-shaped, diamond earrings rested on a velvety cushion. I lifted them gently; the light catching and shooting beams across the room. "They're so beautiful."

"They were my mother's." He smiled. "My father gave them to her on their wedding day, and she gave them to me after he died. She told me to give them to the woman I wanted to marry." He took them from my hands and undid their clasps. I put them in my ears very carefully, watching the walls where they cast their reflections from the fire.

"Thank you," I whispered, tears welling. "I can't believe you would give these to me."

"Why, Kristia? You are my family now."

"But they mean so much to you."

"As do you." I scooted over to him and he wrapped an arm around my shoulders. "You know," he said with a twinkling eye, "I think I could get used to spending Christmas in the country with you."

"Me too," I murmured. This was shaping up to be the best holiday ever.

****

The best holiday ever came to a screeching halt two days later. Ull and I were sitting in the garden watching the squirrels chase each other across the low stone fence when Olaug came walking up the back path. She was supposed to be enjoying the holidays with her family, so her presence could only mean one thing.

"It is time," came her cheery greeting. "Odin and Balder are ready to meet with you."

"Now?" I was mortified. I was wearing jeans and one of Ull's sweaters, hardly the ensemble I'd imagined for meeting my future grandfather-in-law, the ruler of Asgard. Why hadn't I put on something nicer today?

"Now." Olaug smiled. She ushered us inside. I shot Ull a panicky glance as he squeezed my hand.

"You do not have to do this, Kristia." It was a plea.

"Yes. I do." I took a deep breath, shook my hair loose from its bun and smoothed the front of my too-big sweater. It was now or never.

Olaug headed to the library, where she pulled a book from the shelf. The wall folded out to reveal a staircase leading down, lit by wall sconces and carpeted in the softest of fabrics. These waters were too deep for me. I shot Ull an accusatory glare. "You didn't tell me about this!"

He shrugged. "It never came up." He gestured, and Olaug led the way down the staircase, kicking off what I had no doubt would be a very stressful afternoon.

We walked down to a secret chamber somewhere beneath Ýdalir. Bows, arrows, and a suit of armor filled a dark wooden case, kept safe behind glass doors. Another held a sword and shield, each so massive they could only have been intended for Ull's hands. And still another held skates, snowshoes, skis, and other cold-weather amusements. Dark leather couches were off to one side and a large table sat beneath a huge screen. A small network of scanners and laptops was in another corner, while a full kitchen nestled behind us.

"So how does this work? How do I show I'm good enough to join you?" My choice was made, but I was completely unprepared. I had no idea how to sell Ull's grandfather on letting me into Asgard. Especially considering, one, Odin didn't like humans, and two, my very existence was threatening to take away one of his best fighters. Tactically, the latter gave me an advantage. Odin would rather take me than lose Ull. But what if Balder said I wasn't good enough? Then what would we do?

Olaug caught my desperate look. "Just be yourself. They are going to love you." Before I knew what was happening, the big screen was filled with the enormous vision of Odin. Long white hair flowed seamlessly into golden robes and an eye patch covered a battle wound I could only guess at. The remaining eye, crystal blue, pierced through the screen to meet mine with authority. His weathered face was fixed in a gaze that was neither friendly nor openly hostile. My muscles were immobilized.

"Kristia Tostenson," Odin's voice boomed -- the sound of thunder. "You wish to join the ranks of Asgard." So there would be no small talk. No nice to meet you; I'm Ull's grandpa. We were jumping right in. But I wasn't moving -- Odin had a terrifying presence.

Ull stepped to my side quickly, his hand firmly grasping my own. "This is my love, Grandfather, the woman I have chosen to marry." He held up my hand to show Odin the symbol of his pledge, and Odin glanced at the ring. "You do not have to grant her admission to Asgard, Grandfather. In fact, I would prefer you did not. But if you decline, I will join her in Midgard. I mean no disrespect, and I do not wish to upset you. But I am to spend my life with Kristia, wherever that may be." It was a statement, not a threat, and Odin's displeasure was obvious. I cringed as he looked back at me.

"You are a human, Miss Tostenson. It is unnatural for you to mix with us. Why would you think you are worthy to join Asgard?" Odin wasn't trying to be mean -- he genuinely didn't see how I could think so highly of myself. At the moment, neither could I.

"Your highness -- your excellence -- uh. Sir," I floundered. There was no rule of etiquette that covered this meeting. Even my grandmother would have been at a loss.

Ull squeezed my hand and whispered, "Sir is fine. He is still just my grandfather."

Sir, then. I took a deep breath. The fresh air slowed my heart rate a little, so I took another. Four breaths later, I was composed enough to speak. "Sir, I love your grandson. More than I love my own life. I know what the next few months will hold and I don't care. If Ull is meant to die at Ragnarok, then I'll go down fighting at his side. I don't want to take anything away from him. It would kill me if he left Asgard to live as a human. That's why I want to join you. Fight with you. And if it comes to it, I want to die with you."

Odin's gaze softened the slightest bit, and I hoped my words had made an impact. How could he argue with my willingness to die for his people? He had to see things my way. Odin opened his mouth, and a flicker of hope ran through my chest. But when his eyes fell to my throat I clutched my necklace.

"Miss Tostenson, what is that at your neck?" Mjölnir. The misappropriated elfin-made treasure of Asgard. Oh God, no. No, no, no.

"It's not what you think." I tripped over my own words. "My grandmother gave it to me; I had no idea it was yours. I swear. One of her relatives got it from a woman in their village, Ms. Norna, and I promise, none of us ever knew it was stolen. You can have it back. Here." I started to rip it off but Odin held up a hand to stop me.

"Ms. Norna?" He paused, deep in thought. I could see him working something through in his mind. A smile tugged at his lips, but he changed courses again, keeping me on my toes. "You would die defending Asgard, Miss Tostenson?"

"Yes, sir. I will do whatever it takes to stay with Ull."

Odin thought, processing my declaration while my nerves multiplied. A full minute ticked by. When his words finally came his voice was emotionless. "Miss Tostenson, it is time for Balder to render his judgment."

Another man came into the screen. Tall, thin, his face lined with laughter and eyes crinkled in a smile, Balder looked so kind I felt instantly at ease. I stood, feeling ridiculous, for what felt like hours. Finally, Balder opened his mouth to give his verdict. Ull squeezed my fingers.

"Asgard should be lucky to welcome you, Kristia. Ull," he winked, "You have chosen wisely." I released the breath I hadn't realized I was holding, and Ull hugged me tightly.

"Are you sure?" He whispered into my ear.

"Yes," I whispered back.

"Do you, Kristia Tostenson, accept this invitation to

Asgard? Do you willingly relinquish your human life and accept the responsibilities that come as protector and defender of our realm?"

"I do."

"Then there is but one more approval that must be granted." I looked at Ull, but he didn't seem to understand what was happening any more than I did. The test had three prongs: A god must choose a human, Balder must judge her worthy, and she must accept the invitation. We'd done all that. What more was there? "Thor, will you grant your approval? After all, it is by Mjölnir that the magic shall be cast, raising this mortal to Asgard."

Ull's stepfather came into the frame, his enormous stature dwarfing the other two gods. His fiery red hair was unkempt, and he bore the scars of a seasoned warrior. When he spoke, his voice was rough. "My son. Is this the woman you have chosen for your wife?"

"Yes, father," Ull sounded proud.

"Why have you not chosen Skadi? She is the best of your generation's warriors." Oh Lord, there was another woman.

"Father," Ull was obviously fighting to stay calm, "I have never wished to marry Skadi. You know this."

"But she is your equal in every way."

"No, Father, she is not. She is a god. And she is a warrior. But that is all we have in common. She is nothing like me. I will not marry Skadi. I have chosen Kristia. And if you do not approve of my decision, then I apologize for disappointing you. But my decision is final."

Thor's eyes flickered to me, and I held his gaze. He stared for a long time before looking back to Ull. "This is not natural, son. Gods are not meant to merge their fates with mortals. You know this." There was no judgment; he was stating a fact.

"I know the law, Father." Ull's tone was flat. "But as I love Kristia, I cannot live without her. It is unimportant to me whether I live as an Asgardian."

"You would give up your immortality? For a human?" Again, Thor bore no malice, but his opinion of my value was clear. It stung.

"Unthinkingly, Father. She is my life."

Thor looked at Ull, then at me, and back again. He shook his head from side to side. "I am sorry, son. I cannot consent to this union. Skadi is the perfect match for you. A partnership with her would strengthen the Asgardian race, breeding stronger warriors and--"

"I am not marrying Skadi," Ull exploded. Thor's eyes darkened.

"And I cannot approve of this union. Mjölnir was not made to provide a means for a human enter Asgard." The two gods glared at each other, Ull's anger radiating in hot waves. After an endless moment, Ull took a breath. When he spoke his voice was composed.

"I am sorry to earn your disapproval, Father. I hoped

that you would welcome Kristia to your home as you once welcomed my mother and me. I understand that will not be possible." No, no, no. Panic overtook me as I realized what was happening. Ull gave what I'm sure he thought was a reassuring nod before turning his attention to the hushed discussion on the screen.

"Thor," Odin spoke under his breath, "Ull is one of my best warriors. Balder has deemed the girl worthy. Even I can see the sense of approving this request, and we all know my feelings on this."

Thor shook his head. "I am sorry, Father. I do not agree. This cannot be the best thing for our people."

Odin looked like he wanted to say more, but Balder shook his head. Odin closed his mouth and addressed his son. "Thor, I cannot force your consent. And I cannot perform the transformation without Mjölnir. I do not agree with your choice, but unless you change your mind, my hands are tied." Odin turned to Ull and me. His regret was clear. "I am sorry, Kristia your request is denied." My heart sunk. Denied? That wasn't an option.

That meant Ull would become a human, completely defenseless at Ragnarok. It meant that Ull and I wouldn't be able to fight for his family--I wouldn't be able to fight for him, and our fates were completely out of our control. It meant he would have to give up who he was to be with me. This couldn't be happening.

"I understand, Grandfather. Will you still perform our marriage ceremony? It would not feel right for anyone else to do it." Ull's reply came with a grace I did not feel. How was he so calm?

Odin glanced at Thor before answering kindly. "It will be my honor. Olaug, I will be in touch with instructions for the matrimony." His eyes softened. "Ull, Kristia, be good to one another. Ull has been alone far too long." With that, the screen went dark and we were left staring at the blackness.

17. REALITY

ULL AND I SAT ON the leather couch, staring at his armor long after Olaug had let herself out. Neither of us could process Thor's decision. I fought against emotion, doing everything I could to not let my despair overwhelm my desire to comfort Ull. He had essentially been kicked out of his family and was about to lose his immortality.

His father had condemned his decision, choosing to lose Ull rather than accept me. Thor's decision needled my fear that I wasn't good enough for his son, but this wasn't about me -- it was about saving Ull's immortality. We had to find a way out of this. Thor was right -- I wasn't worth that price.

It was clear Ull wasn't going to be the first to speak, so I sat up. "Ull." Squeezing his arm yielded no response. His gaze never moved from his armor. I wondered if he was thinking about all the battles he'd fought for Asgard, all he'd sacrificed. It wasn't right that he had given so much just to be kicked out. My resolve strengthened. "Ull, Thor is right. You can't give up who you are to be with me."

Ull's head snapped in my direction. "Kristia, do not speak like that. You are the most important thing to me."

"And you are the most important thing to me. But your dad knows what he's talking about. If Asgard has any chance of winning at Ragnarok, it needs to have the strongest warriors possible. If this Skadi girl is such a good fighter, maybe she would make the best partner for you." My voice broke over the words, but I forced myself to go on. "Look, I need to know you are alive and happy, even if we aren't together. I couldn't live with myself if you turned your back on who you are because of me."

"Kristia." Ull's eyes mirrored my pain.

"Will you let me tell your dad what I can do? If my visions can help Asgard, maybe he'll change his mind about me."

"Absolutely not. You have no idea the danger you would be putting yourself into. I will not allow it."

"Well I won't let you abandon your family. You have to fight. Even if it means we can't be together."

Ull slammed his fist into the couch. He let out an agonized sound before dropping his head to his hands. "This is not right. I should not have dragged you into this. I never should have let you seek entry to Asgard."

I rested my fingertips lightly on his bicep. "It was my fault -- I'm the one who thought we could have it all. I thought I could have you, and you could still have your immortality. Instead, I've just made a mess of everything. Listen Ull, I … I." My voice broke. This was too hard. "I… can't accept this." I slipped his ring off my finger, fighting the tears. "I can't come between you and your family. I can't be the reason you lose them."

"What are you saying?"

"I can't marry you, Ull. I'm so sorry." I caught just a glimpse of Ull's stunned expression as I put his ring in his palm and raced up the stairs to the main part of the house. Collapsing onto my bed, I gave myself over to waves of grief. My tears flowed freely now, carrying all of the happiness of the past few months. I'd let myself believe this could all work out. I'd even seen myself fighting at Ull's side. How was this happening? The sobbing left a dull ache in my stomach, so I breathed until the numbness came. It was easier than the pain.

After a short eternity, there was a knock at the door. In my haste, I'd forgotten to close it. Through burning eyes, I saw Ull stride purposefully to sit beside me. He propped himself against the pillows to lean against the headboard, lifting me easily into his arms. He took a tissue from the box beside the bed, and dabbed at my bloodshot eyes.

"Kristia Tostenson, you do not get to give gifts back to me."

"Ull," I began. But he stopped me.

"No. You do not get to interrupt either. Now, if you do not want to marry me because you do not like me, or because you have reached the very wise conclusion that a

232

life with me would be far too complicated for you, then I accept that. But if you are giving this back to me," he held up his ring, "out of some misguided effort to protect me... well, then I will not allow it."

"You're not the boss of me," I muttered through my tears. Ull smiled, pleased I hadn't lost all humor.

"Which is it? Is my life too much for you, or are you trying to protect me?"

"Um..." His eyes were endless. Of course I wanted to marry him. How could he ever think otherwise? Oh, right. I'd thrown his ring at him and run out of the room. "Trying to protect you," I mumbled.

"Kristia, sweetheart. I need you to listen very carefully." Ull looked at me like I was a disobedient two-year-old. "It was always my intention to leave Asgard. Even before I met you, I was running away. It is not necessarily the life I would have chosen. Meeting you only solidified my decision. From the moment I saw you, I knew I would give up everything if it meant we could be together. So I am not giving up anything *for* you." I choked back a sob as he brushed the tear from my cheek.

"But what I get is so much greater than anything I might lose. Yes, I will miss some of the perks. But what I feel with you is so much more. I have never felt this peace. Never." He lifted my chin, so I had to look at him. "So, Kristia Tostenson, if I may be so forward as to try to be the boss of you. Do not ever take this off your finger again. Am I understood?" He slid his ring back onto my finger, and my tears started all over again. We lay together as I cried myself out, Ull's strong arms wrapped tightly around me.

"What are we going to do?" I whispered when the worst of the tears were over.

"Well," Ull drew small circles on my back with his thumb. "We shall live as all humans do. We plan our wedding. We take our honeymoon. We live as husband and wife, have adventures, share love. When we are very old, we sit on the bench in our garden, with our tea. If Ragnarok comes before then, it comes. There is no sense worrying about it. But I cannot imagine a more beautiful way to spend my life."

"I can't believe your father doesn't approve of me." Years of small town whispers were brought to a head by the scariest god ever.

"It is not that he disapproves of you -- you must listen to Thor very carefully. He says exactly what he means. What he said was that Skadi would make a more suitable partner to strengthen the Asgardian race. He does not know you, and he was not judging you. Really," he confirmed as I opened my mouth to protest. I sure felt judged. "Darling, he does not understand the value you could bring to the realm. He does not know anything about you, your heart, your loyalty, your stubbornness." He tweaked my nose.

"My visions?" I'd seen myself fighting next to Ull as a goddess. Had Thor's verdict changed my future?

"No." Ull's brow furrowed. "I will not let him use your visions. I cannot lose you. Kristia, it is not important to me to keep my immortality. Please understand that."

"Well it's not right to turn your back on your family when they need you the most. And it's important to me to protect your world. And mine. Just how are we supposed to convince Thor if you won't let me tell him what I can do?"

"I am not sure that we can." Ull's blow was soft. "But let us not think of it any more tonight." Outside the window, darkness had fallen on Ýdalir.

Glancing at the ring on my finger I whispered into Ull's chest. "Are you sure you want to marry me? Even if you have to give up your family?"

"You are my family, Kristia. Marrying you is the one thing I am absolutely sure of. The rest will fall into place." He kept saying that.

"Easy as that, huh?"

"Easy as that." He kissed the top of my head as I fell into an exhausted sleep.

****

Being engaged to Ull meant I got a built-in grandmother in Olaug. As a testament to her love, she taught me to make Ull's favorite Norwegian Waffles. I knew what a big deal this was -- according to Inga, Olaug never shared this recipe.

"Whip the eggs thoroughly," Olaug began. I took

copious notes, much to Olaug's amusement. "Make sure the butter is completely melted, and do *not* overuse the cardamom. You will want to, but the savory should never overpower the sweet."

"How much do I use?"

"Some."

"I'm going to need something more specific than that." Compulsion wasn't a hat one could just take off.

"I've never measured it. I just use some."

I dug through a drawer until I came up with measuring spoons. "How about this. I'll hold these over the bowl and I can measure what 'some' means and write it down."

Olaug smiled. "If you wish." She added the remaining ingredients and patted my hand while we waited for the treats to cook. "You will do fine, dear. You needn't worry so much."

Obsession wasn't a hat either, but it would have been rude to say so.

"I know you are anxious about making Ull happy. But it is such a blessing to see him with you. He just lights up when you are around."

"Thank you. I'm happy with him too."

"Did he tell you I was his caretaker when his mother was away?" That was a surprise. Ull didn't talk about his childhood. "Ull spent much of his youth helping me in the

236

kitchen. I put a blanket on the ground and we mixed the ingredients together on the floor. He loved my spoons best; he would bang them on the bowls in delight." Olaug's expression softened at her long-ago memory, and I smiled at the thought of a young Ull, happy and carefree.

"Ull's parents were away often. Ull and I never lost our special connection -- I stayed with him for each of his mother's absences, and I'm honored to continue to be with him here. He is my greatest joy. As he is now yours." My heart tugged. Olaug had been Ull's primary source of affection. Now I got to be part of their family too, a family Ull had never dared wish for.

"I was so afraid Ull was broken. But your being here gives me faith. That he sees a future for himself, after all of this time... it is a miracle."

"I'll take care of him, Olaug. I promise."

She hugged me tightly. "You will take care of each other."

****

After the week I'd had, Cardiff felt like something from another lifetime. How was I supposed to focus on school when I needed to plan a wedding, make Thor like me, sell Odin on making me a goddess, save Ull's immortality and fight to save the cosmos? Going to class and writing papers seemed like an insanely frivolous waste of time given the enormity of my to-do list.

"Kristia, what is that?" Victoria pointed at my left hand the minute I walked into our flat after winter break.

"What, this little thing?" I waggled my fingers and Emma ran up to grab my wrist. Their frenzy began, like hounds at a pheasant hunt.

"Oh my god!" Emma's cheer trilled through the tiny space. "You did it! You got Ull Myhr to propose."

"We definitely chose the right outfits for your trip." Good old Victoria. It was nice to have one thing in my life stay the same.

"Ooh, now we get to buy wedding magazines! We have to scout venues, choose flowers, colors, the cake--"

"Don't go crazy Em," I interrupted. "We're going to have a little ceremony at the Seaman's Church after graduation. No magazines required. Honest."

But she ignored me. The next night our tiny flat was overrun with thick bridal magazines. None of them were mine.

"Of course she'll wear the satin mermaid gown." Victoria pointed to a glossy page. "The feathers clipped just so on her fascinator." It took me an hour to figure out that a fascinator was a hat.

"Oh, Victoria! She's so going to wear the lace ball gown, the one with the extra crinoline underneath so it has more oomph. And a long veil," Emma countered disdainfully.

"Uh, guys? I'm wearing my grandmother's dress. It's coming in the mail, um, pretty soon I hope." Nobody was listening to me.

Well, it beat thinking about the god thing.

The next weekend, I knocked on Ull's door. He and Gunnar had gone to a rugby match at Millennium Stadium and Inga and I had a date to watch the Sports Wives marathon. As I'd predicted, Inga had become one of my closest friends, and I knew she'd be happy as a hog in a mud hole about the package I'd brought her.

"Olaug's Apple Tarts!" Inga ripped the bag from my hands and flitted to the kitchen, returning with an artfully arranged platter and two steaming mugs.

"How'd you get these?" She bit into a pastry.

"I found them on my porch. She must have dropped them by on her way to London this morning."

"The little sneak. Bless her heart." Inga gave me a pointed look.

"What?" I mumbled around a full mouth of apple-y goodness.

"You haven't shown me your ring."

"Oh my gosh, Inga!" I held out my hand. It was the first time we'd been together since Ull proposed. "Can you believe we're going to be married?"

"It's about bloody time. Ull has been alone for so long." Everyone kept saying that. "What are you going to do about... well, you know..." The god thing.

"What did Ull tell you?"

"Not a whole lot. He's really private, even after all this time. He did tell us you wanted to join up, but there was some kind of issue with Thor."

"Yeah. I'm not sure what to do about that."

"I am." Inga laughed, bell-like sounds filling the flat. "Ull's private, but I have ways of getting information. When Ull said you wanted to be one of us, I went to my dad."

"Of course you did." Inga was a woman of action and Jens seemed unable to say no to his only daughter. "What did he tell you?"

"Odin is *not* happy with Thor. Losing Ull this close to Ragnarok -- it's one of the worst things that could happen. Ull really is unmatched as a warrior, you know." She beamed. "And if you were to fight under his tutelage, Odin knows you would be a tremendous asset to Asgard too." I tried not to think about studying combat under Ull.

"So what's Odin's plan?"

"Well," she bit her lip, "he's not sure. You can't join us without the magic of Mjölnir, and Odin can't force it against Thor's will. The only way you can become one of us is if you can change Thor's mind. You have to make him want you to be a goddess."

I threw my hands up. "How am I supposed to do that? He hates me."

"No, he doesn't." Inga shook her head. "Kristia, I know Ull went over this with you. Thor doesn't think or do anything that isn't founded entirely on reason. If he believes that you will be a detriment to the realm, he'll never agree to change you. But if you can show him you're an asset, especially now... well, then he might change his mind."

I saw where this was going. But I was trying to follow Ull's edict. "Isn't losing Ull enough reason to change me?"

"It should be, but it's not. Thor thinks Ull will come around, that he'll realize he shouldn't turn his back on Asgard for a girl."

"He shouldn't." I felt sick about that.

"Oh, stop it. Thor shouldn't make him choose. That's what's wrong here." Inga sputtered.

"So I have to convince Thor I can help? That's the only way I'm getting into Asgard?"

"Pretty much. Got any hidden talents?"

Boy did I. "Well. Yes. But Ull doesn't want me to tell Thor about it."

"What is it?"

"I can see the future."

Inga choked on a piece of pastry. "Excuse me?"

241

"I can see the future. I can't control it or anything, and I hardly ever see anything important."

"And you failed to mention this because…"

"It's kind of embarrassing." I shrugged. "It makes me seem crazy."

"Ull knows about this?" Inga put her plate on the table.

"Yes."

"And he won't let you tell Thor about it? That's the kind of thing that would make him reconsider, for sure."

"I know it is. Ull thinks it's too dangerous. Apparently, people who see things are hot commodities to bad guys."

"He's right about that." Inga picked up her teacup. "Who else knows about this around here?"

"Here? Nobody. Just Ull. I didn't tell Olaug."

"Huh." Inga stared out the window. When she looked back, her eyes were shining. "You're going to tell Thor anyway, aren't you?"

"I'm thinking about it. I don't want to go against Ull, but if there's no other way to change Thor's mind, I kind of have to tell him. Don't I?"

"Yes. You do." Inga picked up the remote and muted the bickering Sports Wives. "Now tell me everything about your ability. We need to come up with a plan."

18. THE SEER

AT THE END OF January, I returned from a weekend at Ýdalir to a big box on my doorstep. I carried it inside and lifted out its contents. My grandmother's wedding dress was so beautiful. It would hardly need to be altered to fit me. A note of parental congratulations rested at the bottom of the box, along with another envelope -- this one with my name written in Mormor's handwriting. A faded sticky note on top of the envelope said, "Give to Kristia on her wedding day." Wedding day, my foot.

I ripped open the envelope and started to read.

'Dearest Kristia,' it began. *'If you are reading this letter, I did not make it to your wedding. I know you will make a beautiful bride. I wish I could offer you pearls of marital wisdom, but the truth is I just got lucky with your grandfather. I have every confidence that your choice in husband will be just as remarkable.*

Kristia, a few months ago a woman named Elsie joined my bridge club. She only stayed in town for a bit, and just before she left she asked me to give you a note. She may have been a few pies short of picnic, but since I never saw her again, I'll never know for sure.

Her message is in this envelope. She asked that I not read it, and I honored her request. Something about her made me feel that she really did have your best interests at heart. I hope I wasn't wrong.

I love you very much, and I so wish I could have been there to see you as a bride. Keep your chin up and your shoulders back, and enjoy every minute of your big day.

Jeg elsker det,

Mormor'

My curiosity peaked, I reached into the envelope and pulled out a folded piece of paper. On the outside it read:

'If Kristia is to marry a man named Ull, please give her this message on or before her wedding day.' Well, that was weird.

The message continued on the inside: *'Kristia, If your betrothed is named Ull Myhr, then my Ull has found you. Thank Odin! Your union is the key to saving Asgard and Midgard from destruction at Ragnarok. On the day you were born, I recognized your gift of sight -- you are a powerful seer. As a human this was probably inconvenient, but as a goddess your gift will allow you to travel through the realms undetected, to see present and future events. You will foresee the battle plans of Asgard's enemies, and tell Odin how to fight them at Ragnarok. You are to be Asgard's greatest protector.*

Since I was never able to tell the Three Sisters about you, they still believe Ragnarok will mark the end of the gods. And as part of my punishment, I am forbidden from seeking out any Asgardian. But if you should ever need me, hold your grandmother's necklace and say my name. I will find you.

I wish you and Ull lifetimes of peace and joy.

Elsker'

So I was right. I stared at the two pieces of paper, one from the grandmother I'd loved with all of my heart, and one from a stranger who risked everything to help me find my destiny. I sat for so long, it grew dark outside. I pulled my sweater tight around me. Twenty years of crazy visions made sense now. I played my life back in rewind, thinking of all the things I'd seen that had come to fruition. I'd always thought I was nuttier than a fruitcake in a pecan factory, but now I saw my ability with different eyes. It was the key to convincing Thor I was an asset; my ticket into Asgard. But it wouldn't come cheap -- spying on Asgard's enemies could cost me everything.

It was a price I was willing to pay.

****

"She said what?" I could hear Ull's teeth grinding together through the phone.

"I told you not to freak out. She said what I've been

trying to tell you all along -- I'm *meant* to be a goddess. My visions are *meant* to help Asgard. I'm supposed to use them to spy on our enemies. And if I do, there won't even be a Ragnarok. I was right."

"No. Absolutely not, no. I cannot allow anything happen to you."

"Ull, it's not about me anymore. Elsker put this all together before I was even born. You were always supposed to find me so you could change me. We were meant to be together so we could save our realms."

"Kristia, I forbid you to do this. You are not to put yourself at risk. I do not know how I would live without you."

It was hard to argue with him when he said things like that. I tried another angle. "Okay, but think about this. Ragnarok is coming, whether I'm a goddess or not. And if I'm human, according to that prophecy, we're all going to die. So I'm a goner in that scenario. At least if we try Elsker's way, we have a chance at a future together."

Rather than admit I had a point, Ull spent a full minute muttering about how this entire situation was too dangerous and how dare Elsker risk his woman's life for the sake of Asgard. It was kind of cute. But it made me realize I'd have to talk to Thor without him. If I was trying save the entire cosmos, I didn't need father *and* son working against me.

****

I was grateful to see the number flashing on my mobile. I'd been planning strategy with Inga for the last hour, and it would be a relief to talk to Ardis for a while.

"Inga? Can I call you later? Ardis is on the other line."

"Sure. Talk soon." Inga hung up and I clicked over.

"Ardis," my relief was audible, "How are you?"

"I'm great!" Her voice was ecstatic. "I got the lead in the musical! I'm going to be Sandy!"

"Wow, that's great -- congratulations!" I wracked my brain to try to remember the play Sandy was in. My theatre knowledge was limited. "So you're doing..."

"Grease!" Ardis laughed, a happy sound that lifted me from my mood.

"Sorry, I knew that. I think."

"You did. We only watched it, like, a dozen times when we were little. Remember? We used to sneak the movie into my room, because my parents didn't like the language. It wasn't even that bad!"

"I do remember that. Sorry, I've had a lot on my mind."

"Spill."

"First let's talk about you. When do your start rehearsals?"

"Next week! The great news is that the show's going to

be at the end of the semester, after awards season so agents and critics can come to see us! I might get a real job from it!"

"Oh my gosh, that's incredible."

"I know, right? The bad news is that it's at the end of the semester, so I won't be able to fly out for your graduation like we'd planned. I'll make it in time for the wedding though, don't worry." She barely stopped to breathe. "The last performance is two nights before your big day, so I'll catch the first flight out and with the time change, I should be there a day early. I wouldn't miss that for anything!"

"Oh, Ardis! What would I do without you?"

"Oh, you'd probably be in Nehalem working in your parents' shop and pining away for some half-hunky lumberjack," she laughed.

"That is a disturbingly accurate picture of what could have been. Thanks for the reminder."

"Meh, what are friends for?" I could almost see her shrug, and suddenly I missed her so much my stomach ached. "Now what's going on across the pond?"

"Everything. I'm still trying to figure out how to make Ull's parents like me."

"You've got to be kidding. They seriously don't like you?"

"Nope. Not even a little. Well," I amended, "his mom

is okay with me. But his dad is definitely not. So I have this... meeting with Ull's dad. Sort of a last ditch effort. My friend Inga is going to help me sell him on why I'll make a good wife for his son."

"Wait, why doesn't his dad think you'd be a good wife?" True friend that she was, Ardis was indignant.

"Turns out he'd sort of planned on Ull marrying this other girl, Skadi, and he still thinks she's a better fit for him than me."

"Seriously? Skadi? What kind of a name is that? I'll bet she's 200 pounds and has messed up teeth."

"Ardis!"

"Well, it's probably true."

"Probably." I grinned, hoping fervently that Skadi was the first ugly goddess in the history of mythology. "But it doesn't matter either way. Ull told him he wouldn't marry Skadi -- that he was marrying me, and that was that."

"I like this Ull more every time we talk. He sounds like a real man."

"You have no idea," I muttered. "Problem is, his dad pretty much disowned him for saying that." I wanted to tell Ardis as much as I could without violating Asgard's secrecy. "If Ull marries me, he can never go home again. He won't have his family and he won't be able to be there for them if they ever need him."

"Kristia. You know that's not true. There is no way this

guy's mom is going to lose her son like that. She'll make Ull's dad come around."

"I don't think she can. His dad is super stubborn. The only way he'd change his mind is if I can convince him that I'm as good as Skadi."

"Well that should be easy enough. First of all, your name isn't Skadi. So there's a point in your favor."

I giggled.

"What? Just keeping it real. Second," Ardis picked up steam, "Ull chose *you*. He knows his heart. His dad doesn't, and he can't force him to feel something. Especially for someone named Skadi. You know, I bet she has really bad skin, too."

"I love you Ardis."

"I know. And third, you are so way better for Ull than this Skadi chick. You're smart. You're incredibly kind. You'd do anything to help the people you love. You have fabulous judgment. And you have me rooting for you. You can't lose."

"That simple, huh?"

"That simple." Ardis paused. "I am sorry he's giving you a hard time though. That has to hurt your feelings."

"It's nothing I can't handle."

"Don't worry, Kristia. He'll come around."

"Yeah, maybe. Now tell me all about your play."

"Well, the guy playing Danny is super cute -- and he's straight!" With that Ardis was off, giving me a much-needed break from thinking about the task ahead of me.

****

"He's coming -- hurry!" Olaug, Inga and I scrambled into place as Olaug put down the phone that linked to Asgard. It was time. Thor was going to show up on the screen any minute, and this was my only chance to convince him to change me. If this failed, we were out of options. Ull would become a human, the gods would lose at Ragnarok, and Earth and Asgard would disappear forever.

Oh, and we'd all die.

We stood shoulder-to-shoulder in the secret room under Ýdalir, Olaug and Inga flanking my sides for support, our hands clasped together. As we stared at the screen we heard a muted thud followed by heavy footsteps. The sound came from the chamber Olaug told me led to the Bifrost, the passage between Asgard and Earth. We weren't expecting a visitor -- we'd been very careful to keep this meeting secret from everyone, especially Ull. Certainly none of us were expecting the enormous man with fiery red hair coming out of the chamber.

"This seemed like something that should be discussed face to face." Thor's gruff voice thundered in the suddenly small space.

You could have pushed me over with a feather. Thor was a hundred times scarier in person. He stood at least a foot over me, sinewy muscles straining against his clothes and an enormous hammer clutched in his left hand. His face was weather worn and his ruddy skin bore the scars of countless battles. But none of that bothered me. I knew what was riding on this meeting and I couldn't afford to be scared. I narrowed my eyes in determination. I was going to get through to him, no matter how much I wanted to turn and run up the stairs.

Olaug broke our silence. "I am sorry Thor, I did not know to expect you in person. What a treat for Ýdalir to have you. Would you care for a beverage?"

"I would love a cup of tea, thank you Olaug. Hello Inga." He nodded to my friend.

"Hello Thor. Thank you for hearing us today."

"I will hear you. It is all I can promise." His hand tensed reflexively around Mjölnir.

"Sit, please." Olaug motioned for us to gather around the table as she brought Thor his tea. It was an uneasy gathering. Thor dwarfed his chair, but still managed to sit with the agility of a jungle cat poised to attack. I willed my voice to work.

Thankfully, Thor spoke for both of us. "Miss Tostenson, it is a pleasure to meet you. I am sorry for this state of affairs. It pleases me that my son has chosen a companion, but under the circumstances, you can see why I am not in a position to celebrate your union. Losing Ull at this time is a travesty to Asgard, not a cause for revelry."

I wanted to yell, *Then change your mind!* But I didn't want to sound petulant. Inga gave me a nod. "Thank you for coming, sir. I know this is not a good time for you to be away."

"No, it is not."

"I wouldn't have asked this of you if I didn't truly believe that I could help."

"Miss Tostenson, you are a human. Weak, fickle, and frail by your very nature. How could you possibly help the gods?"

"I can't, not as a human. But I can if you make me one of you."

"I thought I made myself clear on that topic. You are not fit to join Asgard."

"Yes. I am." Thor's brow tensed; he was not used to objections. "I am more fit than you know. Sir," I added as his eyes flashed.

He stood to leave. "I have no time for insolence. Olaug, see that my energies are not wasted again."

"Wait!" I ran in front of the enormous man. He frowned as I blocked his path. "I can save your realm."

Thor's snort bordered on derision. "Miss Tostenson, what can you do that all the forces of Asgard cannot?"

"I can see your enemies' battle plans. I can discover

their strategies and report to you. Or I could, any way, if you would make me a god."

"I do not understand."

"Here," I fumbled in my pocket until I pulled out Elsker's note, "This explains everything." My lungs hurt for lack of air until Thor read the note all the way through. The crease on his brow deepened as he read it a second time. He folded up the note and handed it back to me.

"This means nothing. Elsker is a traitor." Thor turned and moved towards the Bifrost.

"What are you talking about?" I jumped in front of him again.

"She mingled Ull's fate with a mortal. She was cast out with cause. Now if you will excuse me." He tried to move around me but I blocked his path. His eyes turned black and he gripped his hammer. It was time to pull out the only card I had left.

"Elsker." I gripped my grandmother's necklace as I said her name. "Elsker, Elsker, Elsker."

"Oh, my." Olaug stepped back as the old woman appeared next to her. Elsker stood four and a half feet tall, tops. Her white hair was pulled up in a bun and her wrinkled skin had a soft glow.

"Elsker?" I stepped toward her. There were a million things I wanted to say, but only one mattered right now. "I need your help."

"I should say you do." She marched to Thor with surprising dexterity for a woman who looked so frail. "What exactly do you think you are doing, Thor? Shame on you."

"Shame on me?" Thor stepped back out of the Bifrost. "Shame on you! You meddled with my son's future. Cast his fate with some *human*? You deserve your banishment."

"You always were a pigheaded prude. Even as a child. Oh, I remember you well." Elsker stood inches from Thor with her hands on her hips. "You are lucky I was not your Norn."

"Well we agree on that at least."

"What are you doing, Thor?" Elsker asked again. "My prophesy for Kristia is true. Her visions will save us. But you have to change her."

"I would never go against the Three Sisters. They gave you one rule, Elsker. One rule. And you could not follow it." Thor's eyes blazed.

"You are right. I found The Seer. Would you have turned a blind eye?"

"The Seer? That is not possible." Thor's gaze shifted to me and back to Elsker.

"It is and I found her. Read the note more carefully." Elsker folded her arms.

"What's going on?" I whispered to Olaug.

"The Seer was one of the first prophecies proclaimed by the Three Sisters, but the identity of The Seer has never been revealed. So much time passed, most of us began to doubt The Seer's existence." I wasn't entirely comfortable with the way Olaug was looking at me.

"What's so special about this Seer?"

"He or she will be able to see everything -- past, present and future. Absolute knowledge of the nine realms at all times. It will be an unconquerable power. Odin thought he was The Seer. He gave his eye to Mimir in exchange for knowledge. But Odin was not the chosen one -- his sight is vast, but he can only see the present."

"And they think that I'm... that I can..." I was the product of an ancient prophecy?

"We do not think, Kristia," Elsker stopped glaring at Thor long enough to look at me. "We know. Even Thor must know, if he can get over himself long enough to admit he is wrong. Touch her necklace Thor. Go on. Touch it."

"I will do no such thing."

"Why should he touch my necklace?" I whispered to Olaug.

"Because if it's the necklace from the prophecy, to anyone else, it is just a necklace. But when The Seer puts it on, that necklace channels Mjölnir's magic."

"Touch it, Thor." Elsker was brave. I'd never be able to order Thor around like that.

"Fine. But only to prove what a liar you are." Irritated, Thor marched away from the Bifrost and held his hand to my neck. "May I?"

"Sure," I whispered.

Thor held the charm between two fingers. Nothing happened. He turned to Elsker, still touching the silver. "See you old woman? It is as worthless as your word."

As he spoke a faint beam of light came from the necklace.

"What?" Thor spun around. The necklace shot nine beams in quick succession, each stronger than before. The last beam was so bright I shielded my eyes. When I lowered my arm, the light had dimmed. Inga's hand was over her mouth and Thor was staring at me.

"Great Odin," Inga mouthed. "You're The Seer?"

Olaug bowed her head, then looked at me with awe. My legs shook. Whatever this meant, it was a very big deal to the gods.

"It cannot be. The Seer is human?"

"I have been trying to tell you this for twenty years." Elsker was impossibly smug.

"And you brought The Seer to my son?"

"Yes. They are the perfect fit. It would take an extraordinary heart to warm Ull's. And it would take an extraordinary warrior to protect The Seer."

"You might want to sit down Thor," Olaug offered.

Thor lowered himself onto the leather chair.

"You too, ladies." Olaug gestured and we sat on the couch while she retreated to the little kitchen and returned with a fresh pot of tea and five cups. Inga and I distributed them quietly.

"What happens now, Elsker?" Thor lifted his cup.

"First of all, you lift my banishment, you nitwit. And apologize." She was a sassy one. I liked her a lot.

"I am sorry Elsker. Odin was wrong to cast you from the realm. I will make sure this is rectified." Thor was sincere.

"Thank you." Elsker gave one nod. "Now agree to change Kristia. The Seer isn't going to be very effective as a human, now is she?"

Thor looked at Mjölnir for a long time before he spoke again. "You will use your gift to protect Asgard, Kristia?"

"Yes sir."

"You will be good to my son?" His words were gentler and something almost like tenderness crept into his eyes.

"Yes sir, I will."

"He has seen much pain in his life. I expect you shall treat him with kindness."

"Of course. Ull is the best thing that has ever happened

to me."

He paused again, closing his eyes as he fought against his impulses. Everything he knew was being challenged and I knew this decision cost him. "Then Miss Tostenson." He extended his free hand. "Welcome to Asgard." I winced at the firm handshake. "Ahh, so fragile." He patted my arm. "Well, not for long."

"Thank you, Sir," I gasped. I looked at Inga, my eyes wide.

"I shall speak to Odin about our conversation. Of course Kristia's conversion will be known in Asgard, but I think it best if we keep the details of her gift a secret."

"Agreed, Thor. As far as we are concerned, the fewer who know of this the safer Kristia will be. Odin shall be fully briefed, and Ull and Gunnar of course, but no one else." Olaug picked up a notepad and began writing.

"Excellent. And I will ensure you are granted entry to Asgard, with full apologies from my father." Thor stood and rested a hand on Elsker's shoulder. "I cannot believe you found The Seer."

"I cannot believe you ever doubted her." Elsker shook her head.

"I apologize, Kristia." Thor turned and entered the Bifrost. "I am needed in Asgard. You will train her, Olaug? Prepare her for life as a goddess?"

"I shall do my best."

Thor nodded once. "Very well. Inga, Kristia." he nodded to each of us in turn. "I shall see you at the wedding."

"Thank you," I called feebly as he disappeared into the chamber. Good Lord. What had I gotten myself into now?

The moment he was gone, I turned to Elsker. "You're amazing! I can't believe you stood up to Thor like that!"

"I had to. He was being inordinately stubborn." We smiled at each other.

"It's nice to meet you. Er, see you again I guess. I don't remember meeting you the first time."

"You were a cherubic baby." Elsker touched my cheek. "I am so happy Ull went looking for you."

"Oh, no. Ull." We'd gone behind his back and convinced Thor to change me. I wasn't sure what scared me more -- fulfilling some ancient prophecy as an all knowing visionary or owning up to Ull about what I'd done. "Um, Elsker? Do you think you could stick around for a couple of hours? Help me soften the blow for Ull? He wasn't very happy with the idea of Thor changing me. He's really not going to like knowing I'm... I'm…"

"The Seer," Elsker said gently. "It is a tremendous honor. And a tremendous responsibility. Are you all right?"

"I think so."

"I will help you." Elsker rubbed my arm.

"We all will." Olaug nodded her assent.

"I'll tell Ull," Inga laughed. "Serves him right."

"And of course I will stay." Elsker patted my hand. "I have waited a long time to see you and Ull together."

"Well, you won't have to wait much longer." Olaug cocked an ear toward the stairs. "He is here."

19. CONFESSION

"HI LADIES." GUNNAR'S VOICE was both a greeting and a warning. "We're back, early!"

"Wait here," I whispered to Elsker. No need to freak Ull out with the excommunicated Norn the second he walked in the door.

"Hei hei," Ull's hearty voice bellowed. As far as he was concerned, Gunnar and Inga had joined us for a weekend at Ýdalir to get away from school. He had no idea Olaug helped us plan a secret meeting with Thor, or that Gunnar had taken him fishing to keep Ull out of the house all day. He certainly had no idea Inga and I had been plotting for weeks to get me into Asgard. Just how angry was he going to be?

"In here," Inga called as we rushed up the stairs and into the living room. "We were just, uh…"

"In the garden! We were in the garden!" I finished hurriedly. "Boy, it's a nice day." Time had not improved my acting skills. Inga elbowed me as she rolled her eyes.

"Sure is. Gunnar and I had a great afternoon fishing." I could hear Ull hang his coat on the hook under the mirror, before he carried a cooler into the living room. "Supper is here!" He swaggered with bravado, making me smile despite my nerves.

"I caught the biggest one," Gunnar boasted.

"No, I caught the biggest one," Ull countered.

"Yes, but yours got away, didn't it?" Gunnar patted his shoulder in mock sympathy. "Sorry mate, doesn't count."

"It counts," Ull muttered.

I kissed his cheek. "It counts to me."

Ull looked grateful. "Way bigger than Gunnar's fish."

"Aw, that's why it got away, mate." Gunnar smiled.

"Stop bickering boys, tea is in the garden," Olaug called from outside. She had busied herself bringing tea and cakes to the backyard sitting area and we gratefully followed the sound of her voice. As we gathered around the table Olaug nodded. She wanted me to tell him. Right now. Was she crazy? Inga caught my terrified look but she nodded too.

"What did you girls get up to this afternoon?" Ull asked through a mouth full of scone. Olaug raised an eyebrow. There wouldn't be a better opening. Why did Ull have to choose this moment to be perceptive?

"Funny you should ask that. Um, well, we sort of had a

visitor." Do it, Tostenson. Tell him.

"How nice -- who was it?" Ull picked up his teacup. It was so fragile in his enormous hand. I hoped it survived my news. It would be a shame to break Olaug's set.

"Uh, well, it was, uh... your dad."

Very deliberately, Ull set his cup down. The china was saved. "Thor was here?"

"Yes. Here. At Ýdalir," I continued unnecessarily.

"Why?"

"Well, see, Inga and I sort of thought that maybe there would be a way to convince him that I should get to be one of you, so we asked him to come and--"

"Inga," Ull thundered. "How could you? Kristia has been through enough!" Ull stood so forcefully that his chair fell to the ground. He started pacing in the small space, crossing from the table to the yew dale and back again in clipped strides. His body started to shake and the veins in his forearms throbbed as he clenched and unclenched his fists.

"Ull." I wanted to defend my friend, but he held up a hand to silence me.

"Of all the deceitful, underhanded things you could have done." His voice grew louder with each word. "*Inga Jensson Andersson, how could you do this to her?*"

"I didn't do anything to her Ull. I did it for her." Inga

jumped up, hands on her hips. "This is what she wants. You are what she wants." She poked Ull in the chest and he shook with rage.

"*She doesn't know what she wants!*" Ull thundered.

"Enough!" I couldn't take it anymore. "Stop yelling at her! Inga did this because I asked her to. This is my fault. I wanted you to be able to protect your family, and I wanted to be able to protect you. Thor agreed to make me a goddess because I want him to. I can do this Ull -- you just have to believe in me!"

"Kristia, how could you ever think I do not believe in you? You are the strongest woman I have ever met. Frustratingly, irritatingly strong in every possible way. You are the only woman who has ever been brave enough to challenge me. Well, except for this one." He glared at Inga. He knelt down so his eyes were level with mine. "But what you want to do is incredibly dangerous. Why would you think this was a good idea?"

"Because she is The Seer." Elsker stepped out of the house. "And she knows it is going to work."

"Kristia is The Seer?" Gunnar clapped his hand to his forehead. "Did not see that one coming."

"Elsker." Ull stood. "How did -- where -- what are you doing here?"

"Kristia needed me." Elsker crossed to Ull. She stretched up to touch his cheek. "Oh my sweet boy, you are just going to have to trust her. She will be fine."

"Elsker," Ull enveloped the tiny woman in a hug, "I thought I would never see you again."

"Oh, you cannot get rid of me that easily," she tutted. "Now did you hear me? Your fiancé is the one the Three Sisters prophesied."

Ull looked at me, then Elsker, then back to me again. He took my hands and spoke very deliberately. His voice held a reverence.

"Kristia? Do you know what this means?"

"I think so."

"Are you sure you want to go through with this?"

"It's kind of out of my hands at this point." I shrugged.

"No it is not. I can take you somewhere until this is all over. Alfheim or--"

"Ull. I am not turning my back on your family. I told you. I want to help."

"And Thor agreed to change you?" Ull tilted his head.

"When Elsker told him I was… what I am… he sort of had to say yes."

"Ull, this is the best possible solution," Inga soothed. "You get to marry Kristia. She gets to be one of us. Thor gets to keep his son. Asgard gets its strongest warrior. Everyone wins."

"Everyone but Kristia." Ull's words came through a

clenched jaw.

"What do you mean?"

"Kristia doesn't win. She has to give up her life to be with me."

"This is what I want," I interrupted.

"You do not know what you want! You are young, Kristia. You do not understand what you are giving up."

"I understand what I'm getting. An eternity with you."

"But you lose so much. You will give up your mortality. Miss out on time with your friends. And you are the one from the prophecy? Every enemy of Asgard will hunt you. They will want your gift. You will require constant protection. You cannot have a normal life."

"I don't want a normal life, Ull. I want you."

"Now, maybe. But what happens in a decade or two? In a century? Are you honestly able to say that you know what you will want for the rest of time?"

"Yes." My hands were planted firmly on my hips.

"You are so stubborn, Kristia!" Ull looked like he wanted to explode.

"And you are so bossy! Aren't you listening? I know I will want you forever. That's the only thing that matters to me. The rest..." I parroted his words. "The rest will work itself out."

"But your family--"

"I will see them sometimes, just like you would see your family if you became human. That's enough for me. Ull, you have to trust me. This is the best thing for us, I promise."

"I do not agree with you."

"I know. But you love me. You want me to be happy. And you know I won't be happy if you turn your back on everyone when they need you. This is the only way we can help your family and stay together. I can't marry you if I'm taking anything away from you, and I can't let you give up your immortality. I'm sorry I didn't tell you I was planning to talk with Thor, Ull, I really am. I shouldn't have gone behind your back. But this is the only way for us."

"I do not feel right putting you in danger."

"You're not doing anything. This is my choice. And it's going to be all right."

"You do not know that," Ull whispered.

"I actually do." I tapped my head. "Great Seer, remember?"

"Ull, you forget yourself," Olaug said quietly. "As the prophecy stands, if you do not fight -- if Asgard does not put forth its absolute best army -- then we all die. Kristia included. Remember the foretelling; our enemies will burn the Earth and swallow the sky. Earth and Asgard will both fall. This is the only way to keep her alive."

Ull's shoulders dropped -- he was beaten. He, of all of us, lived by that prophecy. It governed almost every decision he'd ever made. Conceding defeat, he glared at Inga and Gunnar. "We are not done talking about this." He turned to Elsker. "And you are on my list for dragging her into this."

"I did not drag her into anything," Elsker countered. "The Three Sisters set her fate centuries ago. I simply located her."

"You have to agree, this is the best thing," Inga pushed.

Ull sighed with weariness that hinted at his real age. "If I agree to this, will you promise to inform me of your visions? Every vision you have. Immediately. No more of this behind-my-back nonsense. If I am going to let you go through with this, you must be honest with me about every single thing you do. Promise you will give me every opportunity to protect you."

"You want total access to my head?"

"Essentially."

"I don't know. Some of the visions are pretty silly." Not to mention I didn't want to lose all semblance of privacy.

"I do not care," he growled. "That is my compromise. Otherwise, the deal is off."

"Fine," I grumbled. "I'll tell you about all of my stupid, insignificant visions as soon as I have them. Happy?"

"Not particularly. But seeing as you are so insistent on defying my wishes, this seems like the only way I can have any control over your safety."

"Well if that's settled, I believe you owe me a thank you." Inga was smug.

"I will thank you when Ragnarok is over and Kristia is safe. Until then, you are on my list too." He looked at Gunnar. "Gunnar, you were in on this? How could you do this to me?"

"Would you cross Inga?" Gunnar shrugged.

"Kristia, are you certain?"

"Absolutely."

Ull sat in defeat and took my hand across the table. "Are you going to defy me for the rest of my existence?"

"Yep."

"You are a brave girl, Kristia Tostenson."

I drew a thin breath. "Brave for you"

"You will prepare her?" Ull turned to Olaug.

"Of course. She will be an exceptional partner for you, Ull. I will see to that."

"She already is," Ull spoke quietly and my cheeks grew warm. "I really have no say in this, do I?"

Gunnar, Inga, Olaug, Elsker and I shook our heads.

Inga flashed a victorious smile as she clasped Ull's hand, still firmly clenching my own. "Well now that that's all taken care of... I believe we have a wedding to plan!"

"We?" I looked at Ull.

"Of course. We've been waiting lifetimes for this you know -- Ull Myhr, a married man."

"Well--"

"So naturally, we have to make this the absolute best celebration ever. And who better to see to it than yours truly? I'm seeing a seven tiered cake, gilded chairs, a full marquee with up-lighting..."

Ull raised an eyebrow. "Are you ready to spend an eternity with this lot, darling?"

I didn't know the first thing about what my future would look like. I had no idea what becoming an immortal would entail, and I didn't know anything about being married to a god. But I did know the answer to Ull's question. I leaned across the table and planted a soft kiss on his perfectly pale lips.

"I'm ready."

OLAUG'S NORSK WAFFLE RECIPE

3 Eggs

¾ cup sugar

1 dash baking powder

1 tablespoon vanilla sugar

¼ tablespoon cardamom

1 cube melted butter

1 quart of milk

½ cup buttermilk

Flour to taste (approximately 5-7 cups)

Whip eggs thoroughly, then mix in sugar. Add baking powder, vanilla sugar and cardamom together, blend. Pour in butter, milk and buttermilk. Add flour until mixture reaches desired consistency. Yields one pitcher of waffle batter.

Serve with a tart jam. Or Nutella…

COMING SOON...

ENDRE

THE ENCHANTING SEQUEL TO ELSKER

ACKNOWLEDGMENTS

An enormous thank you to my husband -- for choosing me, and being my perfect teammate. Jeg elsker det.

Mange takk to my amazing boys, the greatest blessings we could have hoped for. Your unconditional love inspires me daily.

Much appreciation to the talented Jacqueline Gardner. We both know this story would never have left my computer without your encouragement. And to Gary Rubin, for your kind feedback on my very, very rough drafts.

To my inspirational teachers, Dr. Carnicke and Olaug -- thank you for sharing your names.

Thanks to my incredible editor, Eden Plantz, who shaped my words with such finesse.

And eternal gratitude to MorMorMa, for making me a part of your family and introducing me to Norsk Waffles. Tusen takk.

ABOUT THE AUTHOR

Before finding domestic bliss in suburbia, ST Bende lived in Manhattan Beach (became overly fond of Peet's Coffee) and Europe... where she became overly fond of the musical *Cats*. Her love of Scandinavian culture and a very patient Norwegian teacher inspired The Elsker Saga. She hopes her characters make you smile and that one day pastries will be considered a health food.

Author Website:
http://stbende.blogspot.com

Twitter: @stbende

ELSKER

Made in the USA
San Bernardino, CA
26 May 2013